HALLOWEEN HEARTBREAK

BOOK ONE OF THE MISSED CONNECTIONS TRILOGY

KATHRYN REIGN

CONTENTS

HALLOWEEN HEARTBREAK

BOOK ONE OF THE MISSED CONNECTIONS TRILOGY

KATHRYN REIGN

PROLOGUE

*I*t's not every day that someone gets to have a famous model, a well-known designer, a nearly pro football star, a trending professional photographer, a journalist, *and* the governor's daughter attend their own funeral. It's especially uncommon for such a group of people to attend when the funeral in question is for a grumpy old artist like Shawn Geiger.

There's something to be said for how a man like Shawn was able to exist in a world with all of these colliding personalities in the first place—no artist can truly be their brooding, deep, thought-provoking self when they're surrounded by not even a single soul who feels even remotely the same way as them.

So, why would Shawn Geiger even want these strange, unrelated characters attending this precious, sacred event of his? Maybe he didn't want this at all, in fact. But once someone dies, do they really ever get a say in what happens anymore?

And do artists find satisfaction in knowing that a lot of them don't become famous until after their death? And if fame does occur, do they even know about it, from wherever it is that their soul took them?

This is the story about how eight unlikely beings navigate the world around them, learning about them-selves and learning about what it means to care about others, as they dodge heartbreak, embrace opportuni-ties, face their fears, and maybe even scarier than that—face the unknown.

Six months ago…

1

DAMASCUS

One year ago…

The bell of a small, quiet coffee shop jingles as I enter the place and step in line to order. I've seen the outside of this building many times since I've moved here to Quincy, but this is the first time I've finally made it inside.

When it becomes my turn to order, my first thought is that the girl behind the counter is hot—like the girl from *Resident Evil* hot. Her hair is in a long and dark side braid, hiding one of her shoulders but exposing the other one, revealing her soft pale skin in her simple blue striped, cropped tank top under her denim-colored apron. Her makeup is minimal, and the fact that she doesn't seem to need a lot of it only adds to her hotness.

"What are you having?" the girl asks me.

My second thought is that the girl behind the counter has a voice that's buttery and smooth, and could put me to sleep with a simple poem.

"Four shots on ice," I tell her, pulling out a five and handing it over.

"Uh, your total is actually six dollars and sixty-five cents," she says, looking uncomfortable at potentially embarrassing me.

Shit, I forgot how much more expensive everything is in this part of town.

I pull out another five. "Keep the change." I give her what I hope is a sexy, bad-boyish half smile.

When she blushes and counts out the change to add to the tip jar, it's impossible for me *not* to stare at the sudden appearance of rose petals on her cheeks. Her name tag says *Jennifer*.

My third thought is that this girl *isn't* hot-like-the-girl-from-*Resident-Evil*-hot. She's more… beautiful like the main character on *Game of Thrones* kind of beautiful. You know, the one who plays the blonde but is really a dark-haired brunette in real life? That's the one. She looks sweet and innocent, and I am finding that I badly want to corrupt her.

"Um, what's your name?" Jennifer asks me. "For the order?"

"Damascus," I tell her. She holds a Sharpie in her hand and pauses before she begins trying to spell it out on the plastic cup. I chuckle. "Just put *Damn-fine* instead." I watch as she fights the urge to giggle at my cheesy one-liner and writes what I instructed her to.

Then she looks at me and bites her bottom lip. It's so seductive that my knees lock up, and I almost become incapable of moving away from her.

"I hope you have a good day, *Damn-fine*," she says to me with a delicious smirk.

My fourth thought is that… I don't know what I'm thinking at all. This girl is clearly trying to be that sweet *Game of Thrones* chick on the outside but is really the *Resident Evil* chick on the inside. The thought of it only makes me more eager to try and get to know her.

2

KENNETH

$\mathscr{A}$s I step off my charter plane and onto the pavement below my feet, all I can think is that I don't want to be in this shithole town.

I don't want to cover this going-nowhere football team, just because one of their players is good and might be trending on Twitter.

Fine, Derek Heed is *definitely* trending these days, but taking on a job this small is so beneath me that it's insulting. I'm a celebrity journalist for God's sake, not some columnist for a big-shot wannabe who's had a couple good games.

Fine, Derek Heed has had more than a couple of good games; he's had more than I can seem to count, actually. And if the ladies love him, then it's a good enough reason for my boss to send me to the middle of nowhere to get the scoop on him.

A town car takes me to the house I'm being paid to live in temporarily. It's a small two-bedroom, one-bathroom—where the laundry room is tucked away inside of a small closet in the bathroom—kind of place, and there's a cellar down below that no one has seemed to touch for years, but I definitely don't plan on being the first to change that.

As I walk across the old hardwood flooring when I first get inside of my rental, every step I take sounds off a tremendous creak.

I run my hands over my face. "You've got to be kidding me," I say to absolutely no one.

It's a wonder this house even gets internet reception.

When I sit down at the small, wobbly breakfast table and set up my laptop and work station, the modem whirs like an old man trying to rid his lungs of years' worth of tobacco smoke, but the WIFI somehow manages to instantly connect. I log into my computer, email my jackass of a boss to let him know that I've made it to Quincy, and get to work.

3

GISELLE

I am freaking flying.

Okay, I'm lying on my towel at the front of a yacht—that's basically the same thing.

"Did you see the look on Stephanie's face when she saw you in your third outfit change?" my friend, Sydney, asks me. She's on the towel next to me.

The fresh memory of me in Stephanie Cordoza's dream modeling outfit as I walked down the runway of

9

our most recent fashion show had felt like winning the lottery. *Oh wait! Getting paid for the fashion show felt like it, too!*

We clearly aren't fans of supermodel Stephanie Cordoza.

"Zees ees dee best day evah!" I cry, trying out my best French accent.

"Paris, here we come!" Sydney joins in.

Our yacht just left LA a couple hours ago, and Sydney and I plan on soaking up as much sun, drinking as much champagne and sugar-free, de-bloating mocktails as we can handle, and doing as much obnoxious singing and dancing as humanly possible during this little vacay of ours. We have another show coming up in Paris next week, and for once, my schedule is mostly open in between the two gigs!

"Giselle, Sydney, shut up! I'm trying to tan," our grumpy third yacht passenger, Clara, snaps at us.

She's not *usually* grumpy, and she loves a chance to ride on a yacht for the photo ops, of course, but Clara actually gets incredibly seasick when she's on boats. It ruins her mood for days. But on the plus side, she feels too sick to eat, so she stays perfectly model-skinny when she does it!

"Oh, Clarie-kins, go take a nap!" I whine at my friend. I seriously don't need her killing my buzz right now.

Sydney, Clara, and I had epic performances at our fashion show last night, so all I want to do is celebrate the victory. It had only been my sixth huge fashion show over the span of my five-year long modeling career.

It wasn't until last spring—when that scandal came

out about me hooking up with that famous guitar player while he had a girlfriend, and I posted the most sarcastic apology video I've ever seen on my social media pages—that my fame really started rising. I was officially at that point where I took a bodyguard with me almost every-where, because most people in the world have finally noticed who I am—Giselle Cosgrove.

BRENNAN

’m a settler, and I very well know it. When Brielle first asked if we could get a place together, I instantly knew that I didn't want to. That I didn't want to be with her forever. But you know what? We all do things we don't want to do. I wasn't getting any younger, and the likelihood of me ever finding anyone more interesting and better-looking to be with in Quincy was incredibly slim.

And I wasn't about to leave Quincy to see what else

was out there, either. I like it here. My job as a sporting goods shop owner is stable, my mom and dad live five minutes away and aren't the kind of parents who hover over or bug me constantly, and I've settled—see, there's that word again—into this routine that Brielle fits perfectly into.

During the mornings on Mondays through Thursdays, I work at Go Play—my sports store—then I head over to the bar by my house and pound two or three IPAs, being sure to test out whenever they put new ones on draft, then I go home to Brielle just as she finishes up whatever heavenly meal she's cooked that day. If there's one reason *alone* to stay with Brielle, it's her cooking.

Then on Fridays through Sundays, I spend the mornings playing disc golf with the team I formed with some buddies I've known since high school, then I either say hi to my parents or go to a bar or stadium to catch a game, then Brielle and I spend a quiet evening either on a date or at home, or we fight about something stupid, and I leave to go get drunk again.

Sometimes, I'm intrigued by the idea of changing up my schedule. Doing something different for a change. But for whatever reason, I can't seem to get myself to do it.

KENNETH

$\mathcal{I}$ arrive at the brand new, ultra-sleek, ridiculously expensive stadium early in the morning to meet the team. The stadium just finished getting built before this season started. The funding had nearly everything to do with Derek Heed, his football playing skills, and his new rise to fame.

I haven't met the team yet, but I'm curious to know what kind of people they are compared to some of the real deals I've met in the past.

"Holy…" I trail off, my hands on my hips as I pause to take in the stadium before going inside.

It sticks out like a sore thumb in Quincy. Not only because of how large it is, but because of how modern and new it looks compared to everything else here. Quincy is a quiet little boating town. The Johnson D. Anthony stadium makes it look like it's on its way to becoming the next Dubai.

"Damn," a woman's voice says behind me. I turn around and see an absolutely gorgeous woman struggling to hold a giant box of what appears to be deli sandwiches, two liters of soda, and a large plastic bag full of individual packages of chips.

"Do you want some help?" I ask her immediately.

She gives me a grateful nod, and I race to her aid.

"Where are you taking these?" I ask her.

"To the team," she tells me. Her voice is like beautiful silk, just like her blonde, waist-length hair. Her eyes are the color of honey, and her legs are tan and go on for miles. "Don't ever tell anyone that you have even an ounce of free time around here, or else you'll get coerced into doing things like this."

I laugh and open the door for her with one hand, holding the tray of sandwiches easily with the other.

"Thanks for the tip," I tell her.

"So, who are you anyway?"

I follow her down the fluorescently lit hallway toward the room where all of the teammates are gathered in. The team has these little events often because their coach likes to make sure they're getting adequate time to bond with each other.

"Kenneth," I introduce. It feels weird not to be able to reach out and shake her hand since the both of ours are full.

"And what are you doing here, Ken? I've never seen you around before."

"I'm a journalist for Sunwest Weekly."

"No way!"

"You read it?"

"Um, sometimes, yeah."

I'm happy to hear that, but I get the feeling that she still goes for our competitors instead. We are almost to that height of popularity, but not quite.

The goddess continues. "But don't they cover more *celeb*-like news? I mean, this is a small college town football league."

"Have you not met Derek Heed yet?" I ask her. She has to know that he's all the rage around LA—maybe even the country—right now.

"Oh, you're here for *him*," she says, sounding disappointed "That makes more sense."

I hold the door open for her again when we reach our designated room, and inside, the team is busy talking, laughing, stretching, and drinking out of gallon containers of water.

"Ah, are you that guy from Sunwest Weekly?" the coach by the name of, Anders Bertrow, asks me, pointing a chubby old finger in my direction.

"That would be me," I tell him, setting the tray of sandwiches where the woman—whom I just realized I never got the name of—tells me to. "Kenneth."

We shake hands, and he gives me a stern nod. "Don't make us look bad, Kenny. You hear me?"

My first impression of Old Man Bertrow is that he should be wearing a white suit and top hat, and doing a commercial for Kentucky Fried Chicken.

"Wouldn't dream of it," I tell him, most likely lying.

My boss, Rainer Wilkinson, wants me to find a juicy story here. And I am going to do whatever it takes to make that happen, because I want out of here and back in his good graces as quickly as humanly possible. Stories like big-time football players in small, not well-known leagues are, as I've mentioned, beneath me. I don't belong in a town like Quincy.

Old Man Bertrow slaps me on the back. "Atta boy," he says.

I know I may only be thirty-one years old, but I don't think I look young enough to be referred to as *boy*.

He begins pushing me along. "Come meet the guys!"

I follow the coach around the room and meet all the players. When he introduces me to Derek Heed at last, I get the feeling he saved him for last on purpose.

"Who is this, coach?" Derek asks, glaring at me and looking not even remotely interested in speaking to me. He's a prima-donna, I can already tell.

But as a fully straight male, I can definitely attest to the news articles and video clips that I have seen of Derek online and on TV, and I must say, they do *not* do him justice—Derek Heed is a handsome son-of-a-bitch. His hair is long and brown, and pushed back with a white sweatband. He has strong, broad shoulders and biceps that are bulging from the too small shirt that he is wearing. I sort of want to ask him if they ran out of the ones in his size…

"He's a reporter from Sunwest Weekly over in Hollywood," Old Man Bertrow says.

"Uh, journalist," I correct him. "From LA." I extend my hand to Derek. He gives it a firm shake that nearly cracks my knuckles. "It's a pleasure to finally meet you, Derek." I call him Derek instead of Mr. Heed because he's only twenty-seven, and I want to knock him off of his high horse a few pegs anytime I can.

Derek nods and says nothing.

This is going to be fun.

6

GISELLE

"*Y*o, superstar!" the photographer calls to me off-set. "You have no idea how gorgeous that pose you're doing is. My camera *fucking* loves you!"

A ray of happiness fills me at his words. I haven't worked with this photographer before, but I am loving him already. Some of the ones I've worked with don't even say a single word to me. I just pose and pose and hope they like it——and sometimes it turns out that they hated every single shot but don't bother to tell me until I awkwardly get brought back in for a reshoot later on.

Right now, I am modeling for Givenchy's Fall-Winter collection of bags. I'm in an all-white power suit with all-white makeup and hair, and I'm against an all-white backdrop. The purses are in shades of black and brown, and they contrast brightly against the set and me.

When I'm all finished with the photoshoot, I walk off the set to talk to my new photographer friend. "Now I know why The Big E is always recommending you to me," I tell him.

Steve Morrison smiles and rolls his eyes at me like he's embarrassed that he's so highly thought of by such a famous person—The Big E. He's still going through his camera roll, and a bunch of set workers are running around us like mad men.

"It helps that you're incredibly beautiful and super fun to work with," Steve compliments.

Steve is a good-looking guy, and he's becoming pretty popular these days in the photography industry. He started off taking pictures of weirdly-shaped organic fruits on a blog of his, and it blew up on Instagram, and now here he is, photographing America's top models.

"Ditto!" I tell him. "Seriously." It's not all the time that I'm eager to hop off set and strike up conversation with just anyone after a job.

"Giselle?" my adorable, tiny assistant, Iris Jimena, calls to me. "Don't forget, you have your three o'clock soon." I love Iris because, unlike my last assistant, she isn't a completely snappy brat who cares more about pleasing my agent than she does about pleasing me.

"Okay!" I tell her with a smile. "Just give me like three more minutes, and then I'll head back to the dressing room."

She smiles brightly at me and walks away, her tablet—and basically my *life*—in her tiny little hands.

"Look at this one," Steve says, showing me a picture of myself.

"Ew!" I cry. I hate this all-white makeup and hair look on me. I feel like a ghost—even my eyebrows are painted white!

Steve laughs. "Shut up, you look like a fucking angel."

I beam at him appreciatively. Steve not only helped me feel calm, confident, and beautiful during the shoot, but he also made me laugh hysterically and feel like I was going to pee myself because of it. I don't want this to be one of the only times I see him.

"What are your Halloween plans tonight?" I ask him. He shrugs, looking surprised that I would want to know.

"Not sure. I have a killer costume and some parties I was thinking of hitting up. Why do you ask?"

"You should come to the party I'm going to." I wiggle my eyebrows devilishly for added effect.

"And what party would that be?" he asks.

"I'm going to Marco Ryder Phoenix's."

Steve all but punches me in the face from excitement. "Shut the hell up!"

I shake my head. I got the invite from the gay sitcom

star himself—Marco Ryder Phoenix is known to throw one of the most *epic* Halloween parties every year. "If you want to come, I'll let him know you're my plus one."

"You're insane," he says, still looking like he's about to crap himself.

"Is that a yes?"

"One hundred percent."

I squeal from excitement and kiss his cheek, getting white lipstick on him. "I'll have my assistant send you the details!"

"You really are an angel!" he calls after me as I start to walk away. "You know that?!"

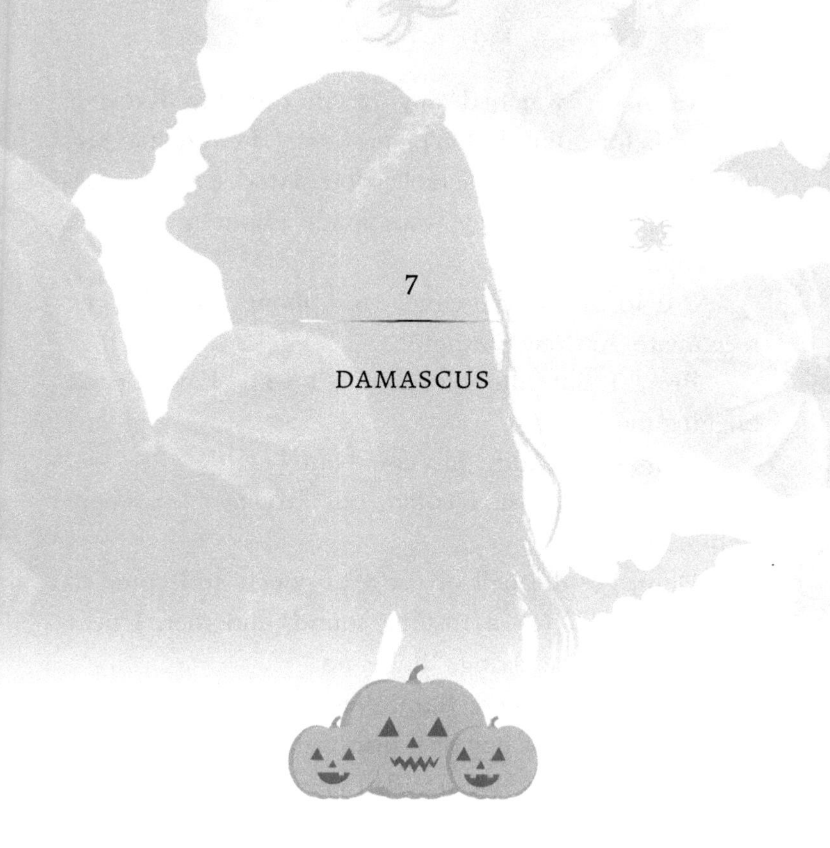

7

DAMASCUS

I throw some popcorn from my bowl, and it hits Freddy Krueger on the face.

"This isn't even scary!" I yell at my TV. It's Halloween night, and I am drunk and alone in my apartment. Do I *want* to be drunk and alone in my apartment? No.

Well, maybe the alcohol part is okay. Only because I thoroughly enjoy numbing myself. It's the only thing that makes being me easier.

I've never watched any of the Freddy Krueger movies before, but I don't know why I even had my hopes up. They're predictable, slow paced, and horrible quality, obviously—they were made about a hundred years ago.

Next to me on the couch, my phone rings. It's my roommate, Andrew Sorington.

"Bro," I slur into the phone. I want him to stop bugging me.

"Damascus, buddy! Just come out!"

"Aw, man, I wish I could, but I'm *super* busy here right now," I lie.

"Dam, get the hell off of that couch and come to this party!" There's a rustling sound, and then I hear Andy's faint voice saying, "Babe, no!"

Then his girlfriend, Sara, gets on the phone. "You finish those ancient horror movies yet?" she asks obnoxiously into my ear. Doesn't Sara know that she's one of the *last* people I feel like talking to right now?

"Ugh," I groan loudly. "Gotta go, there's an entire bottle of Jack Daniels calling my name!" I hang up the phone, but I don't make any move to actually get up and grab the whiskey. I'm still getting through my case of PBR—my go-to.

Maybe last year, I would've loved to join Andy and Sara to their Halloween festivities, even *if* I had to third wheel it while they dressed up in some sickeningly sweet couples costume—this year, they are Velma and Fred.

But not this year.

I crack open another PBR and keep watching the god-awful movie. I know it would only take me three seconds to change it, but I can't be bothered to put in the effort that it would require to pick out something else to watch instead. Andy had been the one who had recommended these films to me in the first place. He loves old stuff like this. I don't know how he got so into it, though; he's not even twenty-one yet.

And Sara agrees with me on the movies not being good.

Andrew and stupid Sara have been together for two years now. They both go to the University of Green Valley, where our apartment is basically on the campus of, and they plan on leaving me alone and moving in together next year when they're seniors.

I get up to pee a little bit later, tripping over empty beer cans, old food wrappers, and whatever other miscellaneous trash that's been left around the apartment by me as I go. I can barely see anything when I turn into the hall and head to the bathroom, because the TV had been my only source of light in the entire apartment.

When I reach my bathroom and flip on the light switch, the yellow glow above the mirror is so bright that I hiss at it and squint my eyes like I'm some sort of vampire or something. Then after I pee, I stumble outside to smoke and scroll through my Instagram feed to see if there are any cute chicks I feel like drunk messaging—there's not—then walk back inside and flop back onto the same exact spot I have been in for the past two weeks.

What a way to spend my all-time favorite holiday.

8

———

BRENNAN

I am the dumbest Peter Pan I have ever seen in my life.

For one, I'm not a scrawny, little red-haired boy… I'm a 26-year-old, brunette-haired grown man. But Brielle insists on us wearing couples costumes every year. Last year, it was Lilo and Stitch. The year before that was Cruella and her dalmatian.

Brielle squeals when I come out of the bathroom.

"Oh my gosh, baby! You look so stinking cute!"

I fight every urge to roll my eyes. "Thanks, babe," I tell her, kissing her on the top of her Tinkerbell-looking head. Then I take a moment to check out my girlfriend in her costume.

"What do you think?" Brielle shakes her butt a little, getting me to chuckle.

"That is quite the outfit."

She doesn't usually wear such revealing clothing, but tonight, all she has on is a forest green body suit with a very deep neckline, and underneath it is one of her push-up bras that she told me she hates wearing because it's so uncomfortable. She doesn't mind wearing it on nights like tonight, I guess.

"Thanks, I think?" Brielle says.

"You *do* know we're just sitting on Travis' porch handing out candy to the kids in his neighborhood, right?" I feel the need to ask, just because she looks like she's ready for the strip club.

She gets that annoyed look on her face—it happens at least twenty times a day now.

"Yeah. So?"

I shrug and shut my mouth. It's not worth starting an argument.

"Come on, let's take our photo for Instagram before we forget!" Brielle cries, suddenly nice and happy again.

The last thing I want is to have a photo of me in this outfit circling around on social media, but I don't know —maybe what's *really* the last thing I want is to start another fight with Brielle right now.

That nagging feeling hits me in the back of my head again. That simple sentence I have found myself thinking about more and more lately. I don't even know what triggered it.

There's got to be more to life than this, right?

WE HEAD TO ANNIE AND TRAVIS' house to sit on their driveway, barbeque, and hand out candy to the kids trick-or-treating. I can't help but notice lots of moms giving Brielle a reproachful look at her costume choice. And a lot of dads giving her an eager one.

I also can't help but notice that while Brielle seems annoyed with me for this or that, per usual, Travis is acting like *he's* annoyed with his long-term partner as well.

After Brielle snaps at me for shot gunning a beer with Travis' girlfriend, Annie—it *is* Halloween, isn't it? —and Travis grumbles to Annie about her not buying enough Halloween candy, Annie sits next to me on her green folding chair in the driveway. I'm on my red one from Go Sports, my shop.

"I guess neither of us can do anything right anymore, huh?" she asks me. Annie is cute, but not my type. And I would never date my best friend's girlfriend.

"What do you mean?" I ask loudly, looking over my shoulder. When I notice that Brielle is standing next to Travis all the way over at his grill, a White Claw in her hand while she giggles at his jokes, I realize I can be honest with Annie; our significant others aren't paying us any attention.

"Relax," Annie says to me with an eye roll. "I know

you prefer to live the perfect little lie that your relationship is amazing, and you'd never want to change it, but I know it's complete bull."

I shift in my chair, a little uncomfortable with how easily she can read me. "But I—"

"I *know* because I do the same thing in my relationship with Travis."

I sigh and look down at my green get-up. "At least he isn't making you dress up with him."

Annie is dressed like Supergirl while Travis is wearing jeans and a t-shirt that says, *This is my Halloween costume.*

Annie shakes her head. "Don't get me wrong, I'd love it if I could get him to do a couples costume with me. But you two are like the exact same person, and I wouldn't want to make him as miserable as I can tell you are right now."

I grin at her. There's no point in trying to hide it. She sees right through me. Most of the twenty-some-things here in Quincy grew up with each other. There's only one public elementary school, middle school, and high school. And then there's the small—but growing in popularity—college, too.

"So, then why is Travis being a jerk to you? You seem pretty decent to me."

She flings her hand up in an exasperated shrug. "Hell if I know. I think it bothers him that I'm not a stay-at-home-wife."

Even though Travis is my age—twenty-six—he's ready to settle down and start a family. His brain has been hardwired to work that way. The McGunther family is one of the largest families in Quincy. He has six siblings and about forty-five cousins, and they all pretty much live here.

Annie has always been upfront with Travis about not wanting that, and he told her he was fine with it. My guess is that they both thought the other one would change their mind.

Behind us, I hear kids giggling, then the voice of probably their parent speaking. "Aren't you two just the *cutest* couple?!"

Annie and I both snap our heads around. It's an older woman, and she's talking directly to Travis and Brielle. My girlfriend and my best friend laugh it off.

They don't even bother to correct her.

KENNETH

I grab the bright orange plastic bowl and a mega-size bag of candy, and walk out onto the porch of my rental home. I set the bowl on the ground by the door and dump the candy inside of it, then I crumple the bag up and toss it into my dumpster on the way to my rental car, a Subaru.

It's not that I don't want to answer my door and pass out candy to trick-or-treaters—I've actually sort of always wanted to, but have never lived inside of my own house, just apartments.

It's just that, well… my rental is tragically creepy and forlorn-looking. In fact, I think I even heard a rumor that it's haunted. I don't want to sit around all night waiting, and then get disappointed when no kids show up. And I'm also slightly worried that older kids are going to want to prank me or dare their friends to do something that involves trespassing or scaring the crap out of me. I don't want to chance it.

Besides, if I head to the festival at the town square and talk to some townsfolk, I might get some *insider intel* —just a more masculine way of saying *juicy gossip*— which I desperately need to get for my stories on the reason why I'm here—Derek.

Inside my Subaru, I start the car, but then realize something; I can walk to the town square from here. My rental is basically right in the heart of downtown!

The weather is nice, so I stick my hands in the pockets of my jacket and make the quick trek, waving at some trick-or-treaters as I go.

I'm transported when I arrive at the festival. The town square looks nothing like it did when I first arrived. There are pumpkin carving, apple-bobbing, pie tasting, and a beer garden. Booths with little fair games have been set up in a neat line down a brightly lit pathway, and there are even a handful of rides—some for toddlers, and some that look like I'd be nauseous the whole rest of the week if I went on them.

"Kenneth Geiger?" a voice asks.

I am standing in line at the beer garden, waiting to

try the local brewery's, Avalanche Brewing, pumpkin ale. I turn around and see a familiar gray-haired man getting in line behind me with his wife.

"Mr. Paulson?!" I cry out with one of my cheesy, lopsided grins. I am quick to throw my arms around my old track coach. He hugs me back with a familiar fatherly grip.

"What the hell are you doing here?" the old man asks me when he pulls away. I smile at the woman, not wanting her to go unacknowledged.

"Working a story!" I explain with enthusiasm. "Are you still coaching? Jeez, you haven't aged a day! What, you're gonna stay fifty-five until you die?"

Mr. Paulson chuckles in a way that shakes his entire body. He is so similar to how I remember him that it almost makes my stomach ache with nostalgia. And nostalgia is the last thing I expected to have coming to Quincy.

"Still coaching, you got that right!" Mr. Paulson says. "I think your father mentioned something about you going into journalism before he moved." He strokes his scratchy, stubbly chin in thought.

I nod my head. Then it's my turn to order, so I grab my beer, instruct my old coach and his wife to order theirs as well, and pay for them all.

I might be reporting in a small town because of a promotion by any means, but at least my pay wasn't cut.

I chat with Mr. Paulson and his wife for about ten minutes, and when I continue on my solo journey through the festival, more and more people begin to recognize me. It doesn't seem as if anyone on the football team is here tonight, which is unfortunate, but I'm having a good time regardless.

"Isn't doing a story on a local football star sort of beneath you these days?" Carrie Hillinger asks me when I run into her on my way to the restrooms that are open to the public inside the municipal building. Carrie Hillinger used to live on my street, and I won't lie, she had a massive crush on me. She's a couple years younger, but I never really gave her the time of day, and then I moved as soon as I turned eighteen, and I think she's always hated me because of it.

But maybe not. She *has* been keeping up with my job, after all.

I shrug at her question. "Maybe, maybe not. Word on the street is that Derek Heed could be the next Brett Favre. Or the next Bachelor." I'm pulling these rumors out of my ass, but I have to say what I can to get these people to give me the dirt.

Now Carrie Hillinger looks more interested. "Oh, really?" she asks me, tapping a finger to her chin. "Everyone keeps telling me that I should apply to be on that show, but I just don't think I could leave my kids. You know, Dawson and Donahue?"

She's referring to her twins. As much as I don't normally socialize with the people from my home town, I still have them on social media. Carrie Hillinger is a stay-at-home-mom—but she refers to herself as an entrepreneur because she fell for one of those multi-level marketing schemes and thinks she's going to become a millionaire by selling lip-plumping lip gloss and getting other hometown nobodies to do it with her.

"Yeah, the twins! How are they doing?" I ask.

I almost want to laugh because Carrie having twins is NOT the real reason why she shouldn't apply to be a contestant on The Bachelor, and we both know it. She is a chain smoker with overly tanned, already wrinkling skin. But hey, maybe in a small town like this, the "pretty ones" are held at different standards.

She pulls out a pack of Marlboro Reds from her overflowing, duffle-sized purse. "They're around here somewhere. Dressed like little avengers. There! That green dude and the one with the shield thing. Cutest five-year-olds you ever saw, I swear."

I try to redirect the conversation, because Dingleberry and Derriere aren't going to be enough intel to get me on the next flight out of here and back to LA. "I bet! So, uh, being single, do you ever hang out with any of the guys on the team?"

I watch the fire ignite in her eyes.

Oh, boy, here we go.

"Oh… of course, I have, silly! I've even hung out with Derek Heed multiple times. Some would say we had a small fling, even."

She's lying. I may not have been a celebrity journalist for long, but I've quickly learned that people will say anything they can to get themselves some publicity.

"No way!" I tell her, feigning excitement. "I hang out with Derek almost every day. I'll have to ask him about you two."

Panic washes over her. "Uh, he probably won't admit it. He wanted to keep it on the down-low because he made a commitment to his team and all that. Blah, blah, blah."

I nod slowly. I know she's lying, and by the look on her face, she knows that I know she's lying.

She clears her throat. "Well, I gotta run before my little Superman tries to use his shield as a grass sled down the hill again!" She sticks the butt of her cigarette into her mouth, gives me a quick wave with no eye contact, and leaves the building.

Finally. I really have to pee.

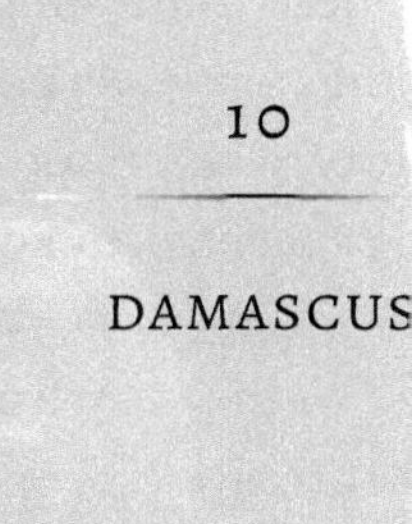

10

———

DAMASCUS

One year ago…

I'm pro-choice. I'm pro-cannabis. I'm pro-straw-banning. I'm pro-same-sex marriages. I'm anti-wall. I'm anti-racism. I'm pro-taxing the rich. I'm pro-safe-schools. I'm pro-free-education. I'm pro-free-healthcare. I'm pro-save the ocean. I'm pro-save the planet in general. I'm anti-war.

I won't box myself into a category just because I feel

a certain way about topics. I don't choose what to be for and against just based on trying to fit into said specific categories. Those are my personal opinions.

That's why I am here protesting against Gerard Reiner, the man running for governor. His beliefs are almost one-hundred percent the opposite of mine. He's delivering one of his big speeches today in Capital City.

I don't have a fancy sign or a megaphone, and I haven't wedged my way to the very front of the massive —not to my surprise—throng of people protesting with me. I'm more of the subtle type. I like to spray paint murals on old buildings in the dead of night and post thoughts and poems at home on my blog, and not to brag, but it has almost five thousand subscribers. In a small city like Quincy, that's a pretty big deal. But like I said—I'm not bragging.

What annoys me maybe more than anything about Gerard Reiner is that he grew up in the town right next to mine, and so he thinks because of this, he automatically knows what's best. And to my dismay, there are a lot more people who agree with him than I would've ever thought.

When Gerard Reiner gets up on stage to address everyone, I yell out the loudest, longest, "Boo!" that I can manage. I think it's fun when his supporters turn and yell or glare at me. I especially love it when they flip me the bird. I don't think they realize they're only satisfying the reaction I'm longing for by being here.

I would've thought that the most disappointing thing that could have happened during this rally would've been Gerard Reiner saying something racist while his supporters cheered for him, or cops coming to arrest us protestors, or finding out that Gerard was now running unopposed. None of those things happened, but what did might have been worse than any of that.

Coffee shop girl. The one named Jennifer. The single reason I have been back to that coffee shop nearly every day since I met her.

When Gerard Reiner stands in front of the podium, he motions for someone to join him. I watch as his wife goes to stand beside him. Then I see his daughter do the same.

It's her.

Gerard Reiner's daughter is Jennifer, the hot, sweet coffee-shop girl.

Maybe the reason it hurts me more than it should is because I had developed this perfect image of her inside my head. We don't speak to each other much when I go into her work and order my coffee, so I've had to make some fill-in-the-blank guesses on the type of person she was. I thought she was the more innocent version of me.

I had built her up to be someone I would eventually convince to join me on my middle-of-the-night journeys to hang up signs over freeways or spray-paint messages on brick walls. I had built her up to feel the same way I do about everything Gerard Reiner is against.

I had never even stopped to consider that I could be so far off.

I'm blended in toward the back of the crowd so Jennifer doesn't see me as she stands up with her father, but I sort of wish she would. I sort of want her to notice me. To know that I'm not on her side. To know that I'm probably not who she thought I was, either.

But then again, I'm confident that anyone who takes one look at me would know what I'm into. I look like a punk. I *am* a punk. A rebel. A scoundrel. Jennifer had to have known that about me, yet she still flirted right back. She still gave me excited smiles when she noticed me waiting in line. She still wrote *Damn-fine* on my coffee cups.

Maybe I'm just misreading her signs. Maybe she's like that with every guy she finds attractive.

Maybe I was one hundred percent wrong about Jennifer Reiner.

11

BRENNAN

I like to think I'm a pretty laid-back dude. While I do enjoy getting into debates with people, I also like to be the voice of reason whenever I see conflict. I tend to avoid confrontation, because I don't see the point in starting fights just because I am bothered by something.

But when I wake up this morning, things just feel different. I don't feel laid-back. I actually want to have a confrontation.

Brielle didn't come home last night. She told me she was going to crash at her friend Danica's house because they were going to have a wine and chick-flick night. Obviously, I believed her… because she has never given me a reason to doubt her before.

Until now.

Late last night, around one in the morning, I got a text from Annie.

Annie: *I hate to be that person, but I'm only asking because he's not answering his phone… is Travis with you?*

Now, I am fully aware of what bro-code is. But I can't stick to it when I am equally friends with both Travis and Annie.

Me: *No.*

Annie: *No? He told me he was going out with you tonight.*

I also hadn't even thought about the chance that Travis might've used me as his alibi—I just genuinely thought Annie was asking if I knew where he was.

At first, I felt like a jackass for not lying for Travis.

But then something occurred to me.

Travis was lying about who he was really with, and my girlfriend—who had been cozying up next to him all night on Halloween—was having a sleepover with Danica. I couldn't help but think it: what are the chances?

Me: *I'll let you know if I hear anything. U ok?*

Annie: *Well, I THOUGHT I was… I just wanted to ask him where he put the garbage bags…*

Annie: *Now it's not going to be such a simple conversation.*

I don't know; maybe I was overthinking things. Maybe I didn't have any *real* reason to wonder if my girlfriend and my best friend were sleeping together. But the more I stayed awake last night and thought about it, the more everything seemed to add up! The slutty costume? The high-pitched giggling at Travis' not-that-funny jokes? The cozying up to him while he grilled? The fact that everything I did was suddenly annoying to her?

I'm a laid-back dude. But I stand up for myself, too.

I'm sitting on the couch when Brielle gets home. Her hair is in a messy bun. Her makeup is old and smeared around her eyes, leftover from last night. She's walking into our apartment with quiet, slow movements, as if she's thinking she can sneak in without waking me up.

But why would she feel the need to sneak back in when I knew not to expect her home until this morning?

She gasps when she sees me, her hand flying to her chest. "Oh my gosh, babe. I wasn't expecting you to be awake already!" She closes the door, and I say nothing.

Her eyebrows collide as she stares at me while setting her purse on the counter. If she knew she was going to be having a sleepover, why didn't she bring an overnight bag with her?

"Why are you just sitting there like that?" she asks me. "Weirdo."

"Couldn't sleep," I tell her, not moving from my seat.

Brielle comes and stands in front of the coffee table. "Why not?" Her eyes are darting from side-to-side like she'd rather look at anything else but me.

I shrug. "I dunno. How was Danica's?"

She shrugs, too. "Fine, I guess."

"What'd you guys do?"

She gets defensive. "I told you. We drank wine and watched chick flicks."

I nod my head. Then I realize I am clenching my jaw so hard to the point where it's physically hurting me, so I try to relax. This isn't exactly an easy conversation to have.

"So… what are you doing?" she asks me when I don't respond to her previous statement.

"What do you mean?"

"Like, are you just going to sit there silently all day or what?"

I blow some air out of my nostrils. I just have to spit it out. "Were you with Travis last night?"

Her eyes widen, and her chin juts out, and finally, she looks directly at me. "What?"

I stand up, too anxious to be seated any longer. "You heard me, Brielle. Tell me the truth."

"I-I *just* did," she stammers. "I was with Danica."

I cross my arms. "Yeah, you told me that, but you see, I just don't believe you."

Her mouth is hanging open as she tries to find words.

"I think you were with Travis," I continue.

She scoffs and rolls her eyes. "You're being ridiculous."

I'm sure she's feeling incredibly surprised right now, seeing as I have never accused her of cheating on me before, but the thing is, I've never thought she would. She had been the one who was always so obsessed with me. She was the one who pursued me. She's the one who wanted to move in together. She's the one who told me she thought she loved me more than I loved her.

Brielle tries to walk away toward our bedroom, like she's done with the conversation and doesn't want me to ever bring it up again. If this were any other argument, I would have dropped it by now.

This time is different.

I ball my fists and turn to follow her, and she heads to the hallway. "Don't walk away from me, Brielle."

She freezes in her tracks. I bet she hadn't been expecting this to happen.

Slowly, she turns back around to me. Her posture is tense. Worried.

"I will ask you one last time," I say to her, my hands shaking and my stomach rolling. "Where were you last night?"

It takes her a few seconds, but she finally lets out an enormous sigh and drops her hands by her sides. "Brennan... I'm so sorry," she begins. But I don't let her continue.

I hold my hand up. "That's all I need to hear, thanks." I turn to leave. My keys and phone are already in my pocket. My sneakers are already on my feet.

Brielle trails behind me and bursts into sobs. "Brennan, wait!"

But I don't.

12

GISELLE

The inside of The Big E's new beachfront home is exactly like the kind of house I am saving up to buy. It's huge, for one, with an indoor pool and a home gym, but it's also modern and minimalistic, and has a bright, airy feel to it.

"So, where is Steve?" I ask The Big E after we clink our champagne glasses together. She's the one who introduced me to my wonderful photographer friend.

Eliza looks around herself, probably thinking she should be able to spot Steve amongst all of the house-warming party goers mingling in her living room. "Excellent question, I hope he got my invite," she says to me.

As always, Eliza looks incredible tonight. She's wearing a chic and flattering Vivienne Westwood dress —Eliza isn't one to wear her own designs too frequently —and the classy black pumps I convinced her to buy in Malibu last week. At forty-one years old, some would say Eliza Leon is one of the top fashion designers over-the-hill, but you would never think that looking at her. Her skin is flawless, her hair is long, blonde, and shiny, and the only giveaway I am able to think of is the fact that she has never once colored her hair, and her gray strands glisten in the ambient lighting of her new home.

I wave it off. I don't actually care that much where Steve is. "So, what's a girl got to do to get a private tour around here?" I ask her. As a close friend, I feel like I deserve to see more of the house than most of her other guests.

Eliza shoots me a smile that's radiant at first, but then slowly curves into one more wry. Then she takes another sip of her champagne and points at me with her glass. "You need to go find my husband. He could use a conversation where he doesn't have to be fake."

My stomach dips with pity.

Eliza's husband.

"Fine," I say, "tell me where Mr. Grumpy Head is, and I will be happy to do so."

"He might have snuck away into the kitchen."

"That sounds about right." I give Eliza a wink, drain the rest of my glass, hand it to the passing caterer, and turn sharply on my heel before sauntering off.

Shawn, the man I am in search of, tells me all the time that I am like the daughter he never wanted. I take it as a compliment.

I go into the sparkling kitchen, where it's bustling with the caterers refilling their hors d'oeuvre and drink trays before heading back out to serve them to the guests.

"Shawnie!" I cry, certain he's still hiding out in here.

Sure enough, when a uniformed worker moves out of my line of vision, I spot Shawn sitting on the cushion of his walker, slowly feeding himself pistachio ice cream straight from the carton.

As I approach him, he is carefully finishing his current spoonful. It takes him some time to swallow it, but I am patient. I put a hand on my hip and tilt my head at him as I wait.

"Party over yet?" he asks me. He speaks as if he still has a too-big bite of ice cream in his mouth, but he always sounds like that now.

"No one is going to leave unless you come out and mingle," I singsong. "What have you been up to tonight?"

A bit of Shawn's jet-black hair is sticking up out of place somehow, so I reach out and fix it for him.

"Stop acting like my mother," Shawn grumbles. "And get back out there and tell everyone that if they want to talk to me, they can find me in here."

"Yeah, cuz the caterers and Eliza would love that." I

take my hand back. "And sorry, but you look like you just got done rolling around in hay."

"Ha! I wish. Anyway, I'm the one who has to use this damn thing." Shawn vaguely motions to his walker. He's probably one of the few fifty-year-olds who uses one, but his ALS doesn't allow him to get far without it. "Why should I have to be the one gallivanting around?"

I giggle at his word choice. I decide to give up. "Fair enough."

I DIDN'T KNOW Shawn before he was diagnosed with the Lou Gehrig's Disease, but apparently, he didn't use to be so irritable all the time. In fact, Eliza loves telling stories about what a charming ladies' man he once was, and how he got her to fall for him that decade-or-so ago, when I was only… fifteen.

I've seen photos of him from back then, and Shawn Geiger had definitely been a heartthrob.

He's a pretty well-known painter, but unfortunately, his up-and-coming fame has more to do with how he can't paint anymore, and how superstar celebrity fashion designer Eliza Leon's husband had been tragically diagnosed with the heartbreaking, debilitating disease.

I get why Shawn acts this way now. He didn't want to get famous from being sick and married to an A-lister. He wanted to get famous for his incredible artwork. And on top of that, painting was the one thing Shawn loved to do his entire life, more than anything, and now he can barely hold a brush.

If I were in his shoes, I would be hiding out in this kitchen, too.

*A*h, good old group therapy.

Said no one ever.

And fine. It's a support group, but it sure does feel like I'm visiting a shrink.

I enter the barren, echoing room through the propped-open door. I keep my head down as I walk over to one of the paint-chipped, metal folding chairs.

"Damascus, you made it!" Terrance's voice makes my insides squirm unpleasantly.

I take a seat opposite him in the large circle and nod my head at him, avoiding eye contact. "Hey, Terry," I say in a monotonous, dry tone. I can't just ignore the dude, as much as I might want to.

More and more people begin to filter in.

Someone tousles my hair, something that annoys me beyond belief, and when I flinch, swat the hand of my abuser away, and look up, I see that it's Shannon. I should have known.

"Still moping?" the forty-something-year-old asks as she takes a seat beside me, like always.

"This is just my face," I lie. I've been trying to convince her since I first started coming to class that I'm always moping, and that I don't even know how to smile. She doesn't believe me. Especially since she's made me crack a few grins every now and then.

Shannon rolls her eyes at me. "Yeah, yeah, whatever."

I use one of my hands to fix my hair and the other to wave it in front of my nose. "Dude. You stink." Shannon reeks of alcohol, but I can't tell if she's currently drunk or just coming off of a binge.

Shannon shrugs. "Yeah, well, I haven't been home in a few days."

Ah, so binge it is.

Two minutes after the session was supposed to start is when the group leader rushes in, a folder and some loose papers in her hand. "You guys, I'm so sorry I'm late!" She cringes. Her long brown hair is slightly messy, and she looks flustered. She sits on her chair at the front of the room, facing toward the circle.

"There she is!" Terrance says in a pleasant, happy-just-to-be-alive sort of voice.

The support leader—or should I say therapist—gives Terrance a warm smile. "I just… had a crazy morning." She lets out a long, heavy sigh, slaps her hands on her folder, and looks around at each of us in turn. "How are we all doing today?"

"Can I start?!" happy Terrance asks. He always wants to go first.

The therapist purses her lips and cranes her neck toward… me.

"Actually, I was thinking we could start with someone different today," she says. "Damascus, how are you?"

I wasn't expecting this. I don't want to talk. I don't want to tell these people how I'm doing. I came to listen and get advice based on what others say. I don't want to talk about me.

So, I shrug. "I'm fine."

She squints at me. "If that were the case, I don't think you would be here, would you?"

"I'm fine, and I'm here!" Terrance throws in.

"That's true, Terrance, but you enjoy coming here. I don't think that's the case with Damascus."

I'm not sure how old the therapist is, but she doesn't even seem that much older than me, in my opinion. I've always been curious about what led her to want to hold this support group. But she says she doesn't have to talk about herself, that she's here for us.

She turns back to me, her face expectant.

I sigh and slide down in my seat a little more, as if

I'm shrinking into invisibility. "I don't know. Miserable."
There. Is that what she wanted to hear?

I'm absolutely fucking miserable.

KENNETH

So far, I don't really feel like I have anything to use for a good story. And Rainer Wilkinson, my boss, won't stop nagging the hell out of me.

"Today's the day," I tell myself when I finish getting ready in front of the mirror in my little bathroom. Then I turn off the lights, grab my keys, and head to the stadium.

I'm not exactly sure who is going to be the one to talk to if I want to learn any of Derek's secrets. I know he has a wife that I haven't met yet, but I don't think his own wife is going to be willing to turn on him.

Although, I do think it's weird that he doesn't have a single photo of his wife on his social media. I have a feeling it's because he is feeding into what all his fans want—for him to be single, even if he's not. Anything to get more fame, I guess.

I get to the stadium nice and early. There's a game today, but I want to make sure I have ample time to walk around and do some investigating. My first thought is to head into the locker room after the team leaves and try to do some snooping around in there. Am I allowed to do this? Probably not.

But I want to get the hell outta this lame town, so I'm going to do whatever it takes.

I show security my clearance ID attached to the lanyard around my neck in the private hall, then I head to Old Man Bertrow's office. He's not there, but the assistant coach, Greg, is.

"Knock, knock," I say with a cheery smile as I stand in the doorway. Greg is a short, stalky man with a permanent scowl on his face.

"Kenneth. What can I do for you?" He's going over the playbook. He looks sweaty and nervous, probably about today's game.

What, do these people think this is the NFL or something?

"Wondering if I can go into the locker room and listen to coach's motivational speech today?" Then I hold up my small pocket notebook.

He's hardly listening to me. "Yeah, yeah, go on ahead."

I fist pump the air, then look to make sure he didn't see it. He did.

I clear my throat. "Uh, th-thank you!" I practically make a run for it before he can give me a hard time or change his mind.

I let myself into the locker room just as everyone is starting to gather around their coach. I basically make myself unseen and listen in.

"You're gonna get out there and kick some ass," Mr. Bertrow says. "Remember what I said. Jennings, don't be a jackass like you were the last game! I know you know exactly what I'm talking about."

The players laugh.

"I'm sure you wish I would just say to have fun today," the coach continues. "But that's not going to happen! You don't want to see the kind of training I have planned if we don't win. Grand Valley is third in the country, you hear me? And what are we?"

"One," some of them mutter.

Old Man Bertrow gets red in the face. "What?! I didn't hear you!"

"ONE!" they all say loudly.

In your dreams. I cover my mouth with my notepad so they don't see me snickering.

They begin their team chant, and I hide behind a row of lockers. They put their hands in and yell, "UGV BEATS NUMBER THREE!" then they file out of the room.

Finally, I am alone.

I do my snooping, peeking into any locker left unlocked, taking notes on anything I might be able to follow up on later.

Derek was smart enough to keep his locker locked, but I try not to feel too discouraged as I put my notebook in my back pocket and leave the locker room.

I walk a few steps, but then pause when I hear two voices speaking to each other around the corner. It's a man and a woman's voice, and they don't seem happy.

I creep forward as silently as possible, keeping my back against the painted cement wall.

"Why are you such a stupid bitch?" a deep voice hisses.

"Don't call me that!" the woman's voice snaps loudly.

"Shut the hell up! I'll call you whatever I want."

I slowly peek around the corner to see who the voices belong to.

It's Derek Heed. He's talking to the beautiful blonde woman I met the day I was introduced to the team.

I watch as the woman turns to walk away from Derek.

"Selena, don't you dare walk away from me!" Derek is still trying to keep his voice down, but he's so angry that he's struggling to do so.

"Leave me alone!" Selena calls over her shoulder.

Then Derek races to her, grabs her by the wrist, and harshly yanks her back around to face him.

"Ouch, Derek!" Selena winces. "You're hurting me!"

Derek doesn't let go.

"You are my wife, damn it!" Derek scowls. "Now act like it."

I stop watching and lean fully against the wall around the corner from them, my chest rising and falling rapidly. Now I know where I recognized Selena's name. She's Derek's wife.

And Derek might actually be a terrible human being.

And I might have found my story.

15

BRENNAN

It feels pretty lame to be twenty-six and living back in my parents' house. I can see the looks of disappointment on their faces every time I come down the stairs, even if they try their hardest to hide it.

"Good morning!" my mother, Laurie, says to me when I appear in the kitchen.

I close my eyes and wave my hand at her. "So loud."

She's cooking something involving bacon. "How late were you out *last* night?"

I walk over to the coffee machine and start myself a cup. I'm feeling hungover and sort of like I just want to go back to bed. But I have to go to work this morning.

What kind of man owns his own store but lives with his parents? I haven't hit rock bottom, have I?

"Just until… like… two." There's no point in lying to her. Since I found out Brielle was cheating on me with my own best friend, I've been consistently walking to the bar right down the street from my parents' house.

"Brennan," Mom says in that disapproving voice of hers.

"*Mom.*"

"You need a hobby."

"I have a hobby." I have my disc golf crew. I already spoke to all of them. They were more than happy to kick Travis off of the team after what he did to me.

"Well, you need more, then."

"Drinking can be a hobby." I grab the hot mug when it's full of sweet, dark liquid and take a sip, not caring that it's so hot I might have second-degree burns in my mouth. "They even make these apps where you cross off all the beers that you've tried."

She shoots me a scowl and plates me up some scrambled eggs and bacon, and hands it to me.

I don't know how to tell her that I really don't have an appetite.

"There's an English muffin in the toaster."

I walk over to the toaster and pull it out. The butter dish is sitting right next to it, so I grab the little knife and slather some on, then I think about how I didn't have a butter dish in my apartment with Brielle. And actually, we didn't even put real butter on our toast. Brielle always made me use that Smart Butter crap, right out of the tub we kept in the fridge.

I sit down at the counter. Mom plates herself some food as well and stands across from me.

"You know, you can sit, too," I remind her. My mother is always on the go, moving nonstop.

She shakes her head at me. "Too much to do today." She stabs at her eggs and takes a massive bite, eating quickly. She points her fork at me. "Why don't you call your brother? I bet you two could find something to do together."

I had been meaning to call him, actually. But my older brother always seems to be too busy for me these days.

I nod my head and keep sipping the coffee.

"Eat," Mom demands.

I take a bite of the English muffin. It tastes dry and makes me worried the alcohol still in my stomach from last night is going to work its way back up my esophagus.

Mom sighs. "How are you holding up? With the Brielle thing?"

I finish chewing and force myself to swallow. As soon as she rushes off to do whatever it is she has to do today, I can dump the rest of this food in the trash, then take the bag out to the dumpster on my way to work so she never has to know.

"I'm good, Ma," I tell her.

"Are you sure?"

Mom's always been the kind who tells it to me

straight. She's non-judgmental and gives me sound advice. I don't ever really feel the need to hide things from her. "Honestly? I'm not the least bit sad about not being with Brielle anymore. I mainly miss my apartment. And I'm pissed at Travis. I just feel like an idiot for thinking he was actually my *best* friend."

"Well, of course you thought that. You were friends since high school."

"You know Annie? His girlfriend of like, a hundred years?"

Mom nods.

"She's into me. Has been for a while. I could have gotten with her any time I wanted to. But I didn't. Because I wouldn't do that." I don't know for certain that Annie wants me, but I'm just angry and exaggerating because of it.

"Because you're a good person."

I nod and pull out my phone from the front pocket of my sweatpants. I wave it at mom.

She smiles, eats her last bite of food—she shoveled it in so quickly that she's already finished when I am still on bite two—and carries her plate to the sink. "You're gonna call your brother. I love when you two spend time together. It makes my heart happy."

"Yup." I find his contact and dial. "Hey, dude," I say when he answers. I stand up and walk out of the kitchen. I like to walk when I talk on the phone. I've always had this habit.

"My little bro!" he cries excitedly into my ear. I roll my eyes and wander through the living room.

"Brennan, go eat your breakfast!" Mom snaps from the stairwell before heading up. I shoot her a thumbs up.

"Hey, when are you gonna score me some tickets to a game?" I continue to my older sibling. "I've been bored out of my mind."

"I'm sure I can snag you and Brielle some for the next one, if you want."

My stomach dips. "Nah, I wouldn't bring her."

"Fine, one for Travis, then. Whatever."

It double dips. "Uh, nope, no need for that, either."

"What?"

I sigh.

"Bren, what's going on?"

16

GISELLE

I think it's safe to say that Steve is not much of a hiker.

I stop in my trek and turn around to him. "Come on, slow poke!" We're hiking Runyon Canyon on this chilly November morning. "You're supposed to be hiking with me, not Bryan!" Bryan is one of my bodyguards. He's purposely hanging back a little bit. Steve is supposed to be up here with me.

"I can't believe this is your idea of fun," Steve says

between gulps of air. When he reaches me, I see him drenched in sweat and looking a little green.

"We're so close to the top!" I say in a chipper voice, wanting to be motivational.

Steve can't help but smile at me. "You owe me."

We keep going.

Steve and I have hung out a couple of times since I met him at my photoshoot for Givenchy. He cracks me up, and he makes me feel like a normal human being with a normal friend, so I appreciate him a lot. Don't get me wrong, I love my model besties, Sydney and Clara, but hanging out with their high-maintenance selves gets a little annoying and repetitive sometimes. They hate sweating for one, so they'd never do this hike with me.

When we finally reach the peak, I drink large sips of water from my CamelBak and look out at the view. It's smoggy, yes, but it's still beautiful. I originally wanted Steve and I to come here and watch the sun rise, but he told me there was no way he was going to be able to get up early enough.

"Damn," Steve pants. "There it is." He clutches his sides and looks over the cliff with me.

I pat him on the back. "Are you going to make it? We still have to go back down, you know."

I look over my shoulder to make sure Bryan is still around. I received my first *mailed* death threat recently, so I've found that I like having him close by more often now. I get death threats on social media all the time, but those are just trolls and people who don't have anything better to do. It's a little creepier when a note about wanting me dead is mailed directly to where I live. I even asked my agent if it meant I had to move. She laughed at me.

Steve nods his head. "Oh, yeah, no problem."

"We need to do this more often," I decide. It'd be good for him. I've always loved hiking. Growing up, I'd go with my mom and little sister all the time. Dad came sometimes, too, but we preferred it to be just us girls. Mom would tell us how brave and strong and capable we are without a man.

Steve looks uncertain. "Uh… definitely."

I shove him a little. "No sarcasm! I mean it! Don't you feel so accomplished right now?" I put my hands on my hips and look out at the view again, my chest out and my chin high.

Steve chuckles. "Hang on, stay like that." He reaches into his backpack and takes out his camera.

I'm surprised but keep my pose. "Do you really take that with you everywhere?"

He nods and begins snapping pictures, and slowly moving around me. Then he instructs me to make some adjustments, and so I do. Before I know it, Steve has taken probably close to a hundred photos of me.

"This lighting is great," he explains. "And that color looks really good on you."

I'm wearing a red sports bra and legging set from Adidas. "Thank you." I smile.

He puts his camera away. "I'll send you those later."

"Good, I need some Instagram content."

We stand there in silence for a while. I'm enjoying how nice the fall breeze feels on my overheated skin and how it smells like actual nature up here, and not like smoke, garbage, and car fumes like most of LA smells.

"So, I get to pick what we do next time we hang, right?" Steve asks, turning away from the view to look at me.

I pretend to be thinking it over. "I *guess*."

Something changes in his face. I can't quite put my finger on what it is. "Good," he says. His voice even sounds a little different, too. "Because I want to take you out."

My eyes bug. "Out?" I ask, my heart picking up speed even though we haven't resumed our hike yet. "Like… on a date?"

Steve's brown eyebrows collide. "Well, yeah. Is that… okay?"

I realize I'm gnawing on the inside of my cheek and force myself to stop. I don't like Steve like that. Sure, he's attractive and charming, but I just don't feel anything for him. And I didn't think he felt anything for me, either.

I'm such an idiot! Why am I so bad at reading the signs?

"Your silence is a little unsettling," Steve says to me after a while. He looks disappointed.

But I'm disappointed, too! I was so happy to have a *friend*. Now I feel like things are going to be weird between us.

"Ugh, I'm so sorry, Steve," I begin, gritting my teeth and getting it over with. "I just… I think we would be better off as friends. Don't… don't you?"

He scratches his chin. "Oh."

"I don't really date." It's true. I've never had a boyfriend. Ever.

"Okay, got it. My bad," Steve says, no longer making eye contact with me. "I just thought… I thought there was something between us, that's all."

I shoot him an uncomfortable smile and tuck some hair behind my ear that has fallen out of my ponytail. Steve grimaces.

"Is it—is everything going to be all weird and messed up now between us?" I have to ask. I hope we can just pretend like this never happened.

Steve shrugs. "Uh, I don't know."

I grab his shoulders. "Well, it doesn't have to be weird if we don't make it weird. Please? I like you, Steve. I want to keep hanging out with you."

He appears to be thinking it over. Then he finally looks at me and gives me a tight smile. "I can try, I guess."

I squeal and hug him. "Thank you, thank you, thank you!" I don't care that he's really sweaty. He pats my back in a slow, awkward motion, then we separate.

I feel relieved. "Are you ready to go back down?"

He looks at the sloping downward trail. "No, but let's do it."

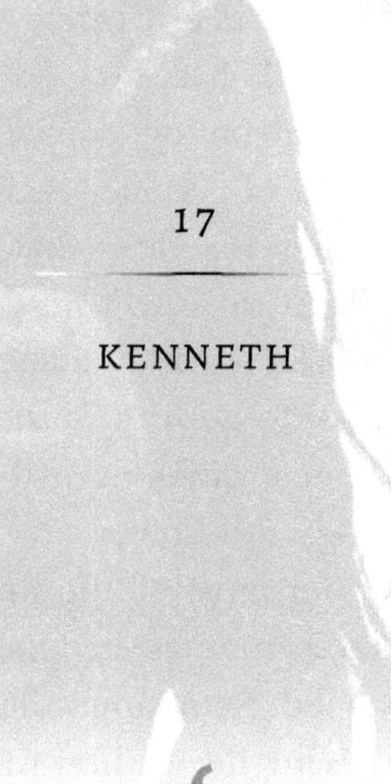

17

KENNETH

Four months ago...

I love being a celebrity journalist. The places I get to go. The things I get to hear. The secrets I get to expose. The luxurious lifestyle I get to live when I'm being flown all over, given access to things no one else is given, and getting to stay in hotels nicer than my house.

I would be lying if I said I didn't have the help of

connections to get me to where I am today. But does anyone really get that far in any career without help?

And yeah, today I have to go interview Mark Wahlberg about his upcoming movie, then make it to my free sneak preview of Jennifer Aniston's new movie before I have my interview later that evening. Then I have to catch my flight to New York City to stay at the St. Regis Hotel—in a suite with a killer view—and wake up early the next day to go to a Marvel film event and interview about fifteen different actors and actresses there. But it's not always this fun.

Sometimes—if not most of the time—the people I interview don't even seem interested in talking to me. Or they're drunk or stoned. Sometimes their publicist freaks out at me for not giving her or him the final say before running a story to print. And speaking of publicists, it can be an absolute nightmare trying to plan times to meet with people. And I spend hours and hours at my desk, at work and at home, typing on my laptop and trying to make sense of all my notes or tape recordings.

It's hard work, but it's rewarding. And I'm a huge people person, so talking is sort of my thing. My dad told me growing up that I should become a detective because of how nosy I am, and because of how many questions I was always badgering him with. I can't help it—I like to know things.

Next week, I'm supposed to interview Justin Bieber while flying in his private jet with him. Then I'm going to a Lakers game, where I have courtside tickets, courtesy of the team's manager.

When I tell my friends about what I do, they practically die of envy. And I like getting that reaction out of people. And with Sunwest Weekly Magazine only growing in popularity, I am determined to stay with the company and work my way up the ladder. It took me a lot of long hours, blood, and tears to get here, but there's no way I will do anything to jeopardize my position and put myself at risk of falling slowly back down the ladder.

18

———

DAMASCUS

*I*f I had known Andrew and Sara were going to be home so soon, I might have cleaned up myself and the apartment a little.

Who am I kidding? No, I wouldn't have.

Sara gives me a welcoming smile, which makes me turn away from the happy couple when they walk in so I can roll my eyes and not be seen.

"You haven't moved!" Sara points out.

I wiggle in my seat on the couch a little. "There, happy?"

Andrew thinks it's funny. I look back over at them and watch Sara slap Andrew's bicep. Then she steps toward me, having to be careful not to trip over a beer can or pizza box.

"Uh, I thought you were going to sign up for classes for next semester today."

"When did I say I was going to do that?"

She raises her eyebrows. "This morning. When I asked."

"I don't remember that." I shrug and try to get back to the episode I am on of *Rick and Morty*.

"But you don't have much time until the classes fill up," she continues. I don't know why she can't seem to get the hint.

I wave a lazy hand at her. "Oh, well. I'll try again next semester."

She scoffs and turns to my best friend, like he's going to back her up.

Andrew looks uncomfortable as he hangs up his keys and kicks his shoes by the door. "Uh, Damascus, dude." He steps timidly toward me like I am an animal that might pounce at any second. "You need to shave. Shower. Sign up for classes. Get off of the couch. Come on, it's time."

I stand up. "Look, I'm off the couch." I'm pissed because I thought Andy had my back. He told me he was going to let me take as much time as I needed. He told me he understood. He told me he didn't care what I did. That's why I always liked him so much.

Sara smiles encouragingly. "There ya go!"

I shake my head at her and walk past the both of them. My sneakers are still on from… yesterday, maybe? So, I open the front door.

"Dam, where are you going?" Andrew asks. He sounds sick and tired of my bullshit. I don't want to annoy him any longer. So, I say nothing as I walk out and close the door behind me.

I wander the streets aimlessly, smoking cigarette after cigarette and trying to determine what bar I should go into.

Then I come across one of the murals I did on the side of the neighboring apartment complex's wall. It's one of my better ones—a pregnant human body with the head of a fluffy orange cat. I had been with a friend who pointed out parts I needed to add or fix while I worked on it. We shared a bottle of Malibu that he had somehow gotten his hands on. We didn't care that we were underage, drinking in public and vandalizing property. We liked taking risks.

Looking at it, I get an idea.

I walk to where I keep a stash of paint cans, under an overpass hidden in some wild bushes in a grocery bag.

It's a little earlier than I would like, but I carry the grocery bag with me and walk back over to the cat mural. I smoke while I mutilate my work, knowing fully well how dangerous it is for me to do so and not caring in the slightest.

I don't know what I am morphing the mural into as I work. But at the end, somehow it's turned into a portrait of Jennifer, the governor's daughter. I've managed to capture that first smile she gave me when I met her in the coffee shop where she worked. She looks shy and interested, and even a little bit wild.

I have a bit of a coughing fit—I think I might be getting a cold—stomp out my cigarette, pack my paints away, and head to drink myself into a sweet and numb oblivion.

19

KENNETH

$\mathcal{I}$ make one of those relieved "ah" sounds when I take my seat across from Derek Heed. Derek is glaring at me like I am the last person he wants to be seeing. I probably am, too. When I was spying on him manhandling his wife last week, he had turned his head at the wrong time and spotted me. I played it off like I had just been waiting for him to free up so I could ask him a couple of pre-game questions.

I get the feeling he didn't buy it.

Derek takes a gulp out of his water jug. His hair is pulled back in that douchey white sweatband he likes to wear. For some reason, the ladies find him irresistible in it. "How long is this going to take?" he asks me, sitting on the arm chair on the other side of the desk I am using to conduct my interviews. It's in a vacant room inside of the stadium.

"Not too long," I tell him, starting my recorder.

"Good, because I have physical therapy."

"How are you and your wife doing?" I can't help myself. I've been dying to get in front of him with my recorder ever since I caught him. I can't wait to write about what a horrible husband he is.

"You want to ask me about… Selena?"

I lean back against my chair. "Yeah, I just feel like not a lot of people know much about her. I know so many people would love to get a glimpse of what life is like off the field and away from the cameras."

"I'm not going to talk about her," he says, shaking his head rapidly.

"Why not?"

"None of your business."

I take notes, more just to make him nervous about what I could potentially be writing.

This gets him to keep speaking. "I love her, that's all you really need to know. And I'm not the cheating type. I will always be loyal and faithful to my wife. There. Write about that."

I nod. "Are you happy in your marriage?"

"Of course, I am!"

"Is Selena?"

Derek leans forward and slams his jug down on the desk. The lid isn't on it, so water splashes out and lands on the both of us. "What the hell do you think you're doing?" he asks me. Then he reaches out and turns off my recorder.

My eyes linger on my recorder, and for a long while, I say nothing. Then I slowly turn my head and glare at the football player.

"Don't ever touch that again," I warn. My boiling blood has to take it further. "Hasn't anyone taught you not to lay your hands on things you shouldn't?"

Derek gets to his feet. "This interview is over."

"I think I got everything I need," I lie, just to make him angrier.

Derek walks over to the door, then turns and points a finger at me. "You'll be hearing from my publicist." He walks out and slams the door behind him.

My fists are balled, and my jaw is clenched. I haven't been able to stop seeing the scared, helpless look on Selena's face when Derek squeezed her small, delicate wrist. She seemed so fearful, like she was afraid of what was about to happen. Like she had been through this before. Like she'd been through worse with him before.

I've never been in an abusive relationship, so I don't pretend to know why Selena is still with such a monster. He could be paying her. He could be blackmailing her. He could be threatening her. But it can't be because she actually loves him enough to stay, can it?

20

BRENNAN

I see her the second she walks into Henderson's, the dive bar that's walking distance from my parents' house. She doesn't notice me, though. She takes off her thick coat and beanie, the tip of her ski-slope nose and her cheeks red from the cold outside. The wind we've been having is making it feel like it's ten degrees out.

Leah, a girl I went to high school with, hangs her coat, hat, and gloves on the coat rack in a way that makes me think she might be a regular here, even though I don't think I've ever noticed her before.

"Another?" the bartender, an old, tough looking woman named Jane, asks me. I nod at her, but then resume watching Leah. I'm hoping she notices me and comes to say hello. I feel like I haven't spoken to or seen her in years. Yet, she looks just how I remember. Long brown hair. Intense eyebrows. Pale skin. Long lashes.

She goes and sits in a booth with a group of older people who look familiar but have names I can't place.

I'm almost disappointed, but then I see her stand back up, her friends pointing at the bar where you have to go to place your drink order. I quickly turn back to my IPA, drain the rest of it, and take my new one as Jane gives it to me and swipes my old glass. She turns to walk to the dish pit, but pauses when Leah walks up to the bar, her credit card in hand, biting her bottom lip while she looks at everything they have on draft.

"What can I get you?" Jane asks her.

"Um, I think I want a pitcher of Blue Moon. Four glasses and oranges, please."

Jane nods and gets to work. Leah looks back at her friends and gives them a thumbs up, then her eyes scan the bar.

Finally, they land on me.

"Hey, Leah," I say, trying to speak in a friendly tone and hoping I'm not slurring too badly.

Her beauty still nearly knocks me off of my stool, even all of these years later.

She freezes, almost with a jolt. It takes her a second to say anything back. "Oh, um, hey Brennan."

"It's been forever!" I turn my body in my stool toward her. She keeps her body facing the bar.

"Yeah, feels that way, doesn't it?"

"What have you been up to?" I'm trying to think of the last thing I heard she was doing with her life, but nothing comes to mind. In fact, I don't think we even follow each other on social media. So, she's a mystery to me.

"Same old, same old," she says, looking away from me and giving Jane her card to pay.

I'm getting the feeling that Leah doesn't want to talk to me, but I don't pretend to have any idea as to why that might be. Is she friends with Brielle or something? Does she hate me for leaving Brielle so suddenly and never looking back?

"Oh, that's—that's cool."

"Cool."

I puff some air in my cheeks and search my brain for a way to keep this conversation going. Leah sees it as she picks up her pitcher and stack of glasses.

I point at them. "Don't forget your oranges." Jane is still skewering them.

"Oh." She waits for Jane to drop the fruit in one of her glasses, then she gives me an uncomfortable, tight-lipped smile—or maybe grimace is a better word. "Well, I'm gonna go back to my friends now."

I nod at her enthusiastically, feeling like an idiot. "Yeah, sure, of course!"

Sure? Do I think she's asking for my permission or something?

I want to slap myself.

Leah gives me one last look and heads back to the booth that her friends are in. I turn back in my stool and have to force myself not to turn around and see if she's looking at me.

"That was painful," Jane comments.

"Agree," some old guy a few stools down chimes in.

I blow some air out my nostrils and nod. Maybe it was just a weird conversation because I don't talk to many girls anymore. At least, none that weren't Brielle, Annie, Jane, or my mom.

Or maybe Leah just hates my guts.

21

DAMASCUS

Okay, so Andrew and Sara had been right. It's time for me to move on.

I think I finally came to the realization after the other day, when I got so hammered to the point where I don't even remember anything. Apparently, I had driven my car all the way back home from the bar on the other side of town. I don't remember it at all. There were no accidents reported, nor did I find anything damaged on my car, but it still isn't a good feeling to know that I could have really messed up—or ended—someone else's life because of my own selfish, stupid actions.

So, I lost Jennifer. It's not an excuse to act like a complete idiot.

I've since then cleaned the apartment, showered, and shaved my patchy beard; facial hair was never a good look on me anyway.

Then I took my friends' advice. I got on dating apps. I made plans with three new chicks. All of them attend the University of Green Valley. They aren't locals. If a girl I was messaging told me she grew up here in Quincy, I immediately stopped talking to her. I guess I'm worried that all local females are just going to end up hurting me.

So, now I'm inside a dimly lit café, waiting for date number one. Her name is Kelsie. She looked cute in her photos. I guess we shall see.

I'm sitting in a booth, close to the edge of the seat so she can see me when she comes in.

A girl enters and slides into the booth opposite of me, a big smile on her face.

"Kelsie?" I ask her. She does look like her photos—black hair, warm smile that takes up almost her entire face, small forehead, and a small mole near her right ear.

"Damascus?" she asks back.

"That's me."

She giggles. "I had to Google how to pronounce your name. Haven't heard that one before.

Instantly, I'm taken back to when Jennifer struggled to spell my name on the first cup of coffee I ever ordered from her. My stomach lurches so largely that I get dizzy.

I nod and smile at the girl, trying to fight through the pain.

Somehow, I make it through the entire date. But I won't be calling her or texting her again. Her dark hair. Her slightly chipped nail polish, the way she didn't like her foods touching each other on her plate. The way she kept tilting her head down and looking at me through her lashes, trying to be seductive and cute. I couldn't handle it. It was all so… Jennifer.

I go home and go right to bed, because if I'm not going to drink, then sleeping is the next best way to numb myself.

I WAKE up the next day and try again, with girl number two. I try telling Andrew I don't think I should, but he somehow convinces me.

"Try not to think about your ex this time. It's not healthy to compare people!" he calls to me as I head out of the apartment and down the stairs to my car.

This date is at a pool hall right on the other side of campus. It used to be full of old bikers, but the college kids have since taken it over, and now I'm pretty sure it turns into a nightclub on the weekends.

Girl number two is Kimber. She's a blonde, at least, so I don't think I'll find too many similarities to Jennifer when I meet her.

I meet Kimber inside, give her a friendly hug,

compliment how pretty she is, and walk us to the bar so I can buy her a drink.

I smile at my pretty blonde date. "What are you having?"

"Anything but whiskey!" she says, making a face of disgust.

Damn.

It's the same face Jennifer made whenever she got too close to any dark-colored whiskey drink.

"N-not a whiskey fan?" I stammer.

"Let's just say the first time I had it will be the last, I think."

I'm pretty sure Jennifer told me the exact same thing. But I nod my head anyway. I can do this.

We get our drinks, find a pool table, and get our sticks ready. When it's her turn, she sticks her tongue out in concentration.

Just.

Like.

Jennifer.

I tell her I suddenly don't feel well and haul out of that building like my life depends on it.

WHEN DATE THREE ROLLS AROUND, I drive away as soon as I pull into the parking lot outside the coffee shop and see her. She was wearing the exact same floral blouse that Jennifer used to have. I don't even bother to message her and explain. In fact, I just delete all and any dating apps I have installed on my phone.

"You don't understand," I complain to Andrew and Sara when I'm lying across the couch later. "It's like I'm destined to only date girls who remind me of her. It's fucking impossible!"

Sara sits on the arm of the couch by my feet. "Maybe you just need to change your taste in women," she suggests.

"I thought I did! I chose two blonde girls!"

"Yeah, but all three girls you tried to date looked like they wanted to ruin your life in their photos."

I forgot I had shown Sara their pictures. "What? No way!" I sit up.

"Yeah! They all looked like they had serious daddy issues! Tell my I'm right, babe." She's referring to Andrew, who is sitting on the loveseat next to the cushion with the huge tear in it.

Andrew shrugs. "She does have a point."

I groan.

"I have an idea!" Sara jumps off of the arm rest and wiggles her eyebrows. "I don't know why I didn't think of it sooner!"

"Where are you going?" Andrew asks as she heads to the door to leave.

"I'll call you and tell you the plan later! Just know that I am a total genius!"

22

GISELLE

I'm in The Big E's glorious, sky-high office. She invited me here. She wants me to model some designs that she has been working on. "You're the only one I can trust," she had told me over the phone.

"If you don't keep still, I won't hesitate to stick this pin in you," Eliza says to me. One of her assistants swallows visibly and gets a horrified expression on her face like she thinks Eliza means it.

I don't get why people are so scared of Eliza Leon.

Sure, she's super famous and amazingly talented and might come off as a little intimidating, but anyone who knows her quickly learns that she's the biggest softie in the world. She genuinely wants the best for everyone. Her kindness, compassion, and consideration for others are just a few of the things I love about her.

"Yeah, E. Get some blood on the fabric. That will really add to the overall look," I joke, standing on her pedestal while she's crouched at my knees, pinning two pieces of fabric together and growling loudly when she doesn't like how it looks.

She snaps her head to her assistant, who immediately straightens up. "Macy, I need more of that silvery fabric. Do you know what I'm talking about?"

Her assistant nods like even if she didn't know, she would never admit it to her. Eliza dismisses her, then looks at my assistant. "Can she be free for another hour?"

Even poor little Iris is thrown off by Eliza's snappy voice. She doesn't realize—and neither does that Macy chick, I don't think—that that's just how Eliza sounds. She's not being mean; she just doesn't like wasting time.

"Uh, I can check…" Iris taps on my tablet with her stylus. "She does have something scheduled." She looks up at Eliza.

Then she keeps tapping away.

"But I think I should be able to move some things around," she continues. "I just have to make some calls…"

"Excellent!" Eliza smiles brightly. Iris excuses herself and leaves Eliza and I alone in her office.

Eliza gets to her feet and smooths her skirt. "If I don't get this design just right, you might as well consider my career finished." She lets out a heavy sigh and begins unpinning me.

"What are you doing?" Normally, I would stay dead silent if a designer was using me as a body to work of off, but since Eliza is a friend, I feel like I'm allowed to ask.

"Starting from scratch." Eliza looks flustered and frazzled, and I think maybe she could use a couple of deep breaths and a glass of water. So, I take her shoulders and still her busy body.

She looks up at me on my pedestal in surprise.

"I think we should take five, don't you?"

She holds out her hand and lets me step down. "Fine, just don't sit down, or you'll get a pin in your ass."

We both giggle. When I catch her eye again, I can already tell that she's feeling a little lighter. It's like they say—laughter is the best medicine.

My eyes go to my hand, which is still held in hers even though I'm safely on the ground. I don't attempt to remove it, but when Eliza sees it, she casually lets go and fluffs her hair.

"I'm just feeling so pressured right now. And Shawn's doctor's appointment didn't exactly go smoothly yesterday, and watching my beautiful new bathroom be remodeled to be compliant with Shawn's future needs..." She takes a seat in her desk chair. "I guess I just feel like I aged twenty years in the span of a few months."

"That does sound like a lot." I stay standing but walk —in tiny steps because it's all the pins will allow—over to her.

"And I feel like a horrible person for even being upset in the first place. It's not as if I'm the one with the disease."

"You're allowed to be upset for whatever you want to be upset about. It's not a contest of who has more reason to hurt."

She barks a pitiful laugh. "Twenty-five years old and yet, you are so much wiser than me, Giselle."

"Oh, please." I roll my eyes. "You're not even that much older than me."

She waves a well-manicured and moisturized hand at me. "No compliments. I haven't earned any yet today."

"It was a fact, not a compliment."

And I mean it, too. Fifteen years and three months —yes, I've counted—isn't really that far apart in the grand scheme of things. I have never looked at Eliza as a mother, aunt, or elder. I've always seen her as my equal.

She smiles at me. "I can see why Shawn jokes about wanting to adopt you."

I internally sigh. I might see her as my equal, but she clearly doesn't feel the same way.

23

KENNETH

It might be close to freezing and windy as fuck outside, but that isn't stopping what seems like the entire town of Quincy from being at this football game. I'm watching from up in the stands, but I'm leaned against the railing for the best viewpoint. I have access to anywhere I want to go, even the sidelines, but I'm on the lookout for any Derek fans that seem like they might be related to him.

It doesn't take long before I hear a loud, angry

sounding, "Hey!" in the distance. I turn to my left and see none other than Selena Heed herself. She is stomping toward me. I think she might be trying to glare at me, but her teeth are chattering from the cold, and the wind is blowing in the opposite direction so her long blonde hair keeps blowing in front of her face. She angrily swats at her mane and squeezes in between me and the stranger next to me. She puts a gloved hand on the railing and points the other in my face.

"What were you interviewing my husband about?" she demands. I'm surprised. If I'm being honest, I would have thought someone finally pointing out to Derek that they know how horribly he treats her would have made Selena thankful for me, not angry.

I guess I had been wrong.

"Why? What did he tell you?" I reply. As the journalist, I'm the one who gets to ask questions.

She doesn't answer it. "I don't know why you think you can come here and—" the team scores a touchdown so the crowd around us goes nuts, and we have to wait a moment for them to calm down, "—and start making wild accusations and inserting yourself where you don't belong."

I turn my body away from the field and toward her. "Look, I don't know what story Derek somehow managed to put in your head, but I know what I saw by that locker room."

I wonder how many years Derek has spent manipulating her. "Selena… how he talks to you, how he touches you? It's not okay!"

She hisses. "K-keep your voice d-down!" Her teeth

are still chattering violently. "You have no idea what you're talking about. You have no idea what you saw."

I'm not buying it. I reach out to place a hand on her shoulder. The way she flinches and squeezes her eyes shut, even though it's only for a split second, makes me recoil. I feel just as bad as if I *had* intentionally hurt her, like she clearly thought I had just been about to.

Right in this moment, all I want to do is help her. I want to help her escape from Derek more than I want to get a good story out of it.

She composes herself and holds her shaking head up high. "Do us all a favor and just… go back to wherever you came from, okay?"

I open my mouth to reply, to tell her that she doesn't have to be afraid anymore, but she turns and walks away before I can.

24

DAMASCUS

’m at the pool hall again. This time, it’s with
Andrew. Luckily, girl number two isn’t here to
ask me why I suddenly started ghosting her. Sara’s plan
was that she was going to go pick up her friend and
meet us here. She was going to make it out to be just a
casual thing. That way, I didn’t feel the pressure of being
on a date, and her friend didn’t feel like she was being
set up with some random dude.

When the friend she brings, Blair, first walks in, my

eyes widen. She's definitely beautiful, yes. But I'm more surprised by the shock of reddish-orange hair that she has. I've never dated a ginger. I always assumed they were crazy.

But Blair doesn't look crazy. I know looks can be deceiving, but with her plain, light makeup, simple jeans, a slightly cropped t-shirt, and clean white sneakers, she looks pretty much harmless. I would have scrolled past her on a dating app, I think. Mainly because of the hair color.

But maybe Sara was right; maybe I do need to branch out and change my taste.

They reach us, Sara smiling eagerly, and Blair smiling more reserved-like.

Sara kisses Andrew, then motions between us and her friend. "This is Blair. We have Math 205 together. Blair, this is my boyfriend, Andrew, and his friend, Damascus."

Blair gives us a small, awkward wave. "Hello," she says, her voice stronger than I was imagining it sounding. "I've heard a lot about you, Andrew." Then she looks at me next. Her blue eyes are bright and bold and almost shock me. "Do you go to UGV, too?"

"Nope, I'm a dropout."

She has to know exactly who she's dealing with before she decides she thinks I might maybe be good enough for. Just by looking at her, I get the sense that she needs a Harvard-going, I'm-going-to-be-a-doctor kind of guy.

But Blair shrugs. "Good for you. It's stupid-expensive anyway."

I'm so thrown off that I actually chuckle a little.

"It *is*, right?" I can't help but say back.

Sara cuts in. "So, who is going to get us drinks?"

"I can," Blair and I say together. Then she looks at me. "Well, I don't turn twenty-one for a couple of months, but I have my fake with me."

How can someone who looks so innocent have a fake ID and red hair? Blair is a total mystery to me. But maybe a mystery is exactly what I need. Because for the first time in about one year and six months, I haven't thought of Jennifer Reiner for over thirty seconds.

25

BRENNAN

It's the first Thanksgiving I've had without Brielle or having to see her parents in… a while. I'm surprised that I don't even feel sad about it. I don't miss house-hopping, having dinner at one place, dessert at another, and arguing with each other about what order we did it the year before.

"Brennan!" Mom calls from downstairs. I'm in my bathroom, finishing up getting ready for the day. I have on my mom's favorite sweater of mine and my nice beige slacks. My favorite sneakers are on my feet, though; she's not going to ever convince me that I have to wear dress shoes just to hang around the house with my family all day. "Get down here and help me!"

"Brennan!" my dad, Richard, joins in.

I groan loudly. "I'm coming!"

Another thing I don't miss—living in this house and being coerced into helping get the evening ready. When I had the apartment with Brielle, all I had to do was show up and eat.

I get downstairs and plaster a smile on my face. "Happy Thanksgiving!" I tell my parents while going around the kitchen and hugging them. Dad smiles pleasantly after our hug breaks apart and cracks the turkey open to check on it.

"Not too much longer," he says in an excited voice. Dad loves cooking turkeys. He has since I was a kid. Every year, it seems like he has a different marinade or seasoning recipe to use on it.

"What time are we eating?" I ask, looking at the clock on the stove. It's only one in the afternoon.

"Four!" Mom and Dad say together, Mom's tone annoyed like she's told me this a hundred times. She probably has.

I hold my hands up in surrender. "Sorry, sorry," I say, looking around the disastrous kitchen. "What can I do?"

"Your brother will be here in about an hour, so focus on making sure the house looks nice and the snacks are set up, would you?" Mom instructs.

I do as I'm told, excited to see my older brother. The last two years, he couldn't come, and now that I didn't have Brielle around to nag in my ear about how she wanted to leave soon, I could relax and actually have some fun with him.

Only forty-five minutes late, the person I am assuming is my brother knocks on the front door. It sort of weirds me out that he doesn't just let himself in, but when I walk to the foyer, I realize the door is locked.

When I open it, the grin on my face nearly falters a little. It definitely is my older brother.

But it's also his wife.

"Brennan!" Derek cries, punching me brotherly-like in the chest and pushing his way in. He gives me a hug and messes up my hair, so I sock him in the stomach. I don't know if we're ever going to outgrow the play-fighting.

"Killer win today!" I congratulate him. He's an incredible football player who I have no doubt is going to be going pro any day now.

"Is that my handsome son I hear?" Mom calls, her and Dad still in the kitchen.

"Yes," Derek and I say at the same time. Next to him, Selena, his wife, takes her jacket off and hangs it on the rack by the door. Then she turns and gives me a friendly smile.

"Good to see you, Brennan," she says, not making a move to hug me. I don't make the move to hug her, either. Instead, I just nod my head and put the fake smile on.

"Yeah, you too," I lie. No one had mentioned

anything to me about Derek's wife coming to Thanksgiving, but I guess since they're married, it's sort of expected. She had traveled with her family somewhere the last couple of times for the holiday, so I guess I had been expecting that to happen this year, too.

It's not that I don't like Selena…

Okay, it is. Sue me.

"Get in here and give me a hug!" Mom calls.

Derek heads to the kitchen, and not wanting to be left alone in the foyer with Selena, I follow him.

Mom and Dad take their turns hugging their son and complimenting him on his game this morning. We had watched it on TV.

"Bren, you should've come!" Derek complains, stealing a piece of celery and shoveling it into his mouth. He has on Mom's favorite sweater of his, too, like we do for her every year. His is army green and has a classic holiday pattern threaded into it. Mine is striped with muted, fall colors. Mom says it makes my eyes pop.

Mom swats Derek's hand and shoos him. "No, Brennan should not have gone," she argues. "We needed his help here. And there are snacks in the living room!"

"You're the one who told me to come in here in the first place!"

Mom looks around Derek. "Where's Selena?"

"Babe!" Derek shouts. Seconds later, Selena appears in the kitchen.

She really waited until she was invited to join in? I fight the urge to roll my eyes at her.

Mom and Dad hug her next, and the three of them

catch up briefly while I wait for them to finish, so Derek and I can crack open some beers and watch some football in the living room until it's time to eat.

26

—

GISELLE

"Happy Thanksgiving, Bee!" I say to my little sister, who still lives back home.

"Thanks, Gee!" she replies. I call her Bee, and she calls me Gee. When we're together, we call ourselves the BeeGees. "I wish you were here."

"I wish *you* were *here*," I deadpan. "You'd freaking love it here, Bee. Why haven't you come out to see me yet? There's so much I want to show you!" I've only been begging her to come out and visit me since I first

119

moved out here, practically. But my sister is annoyingly smart and wants to graduate college and blah, blah, blah.

"I will soon," she tells me. I'm in my bedroom in my apartment, fresh out of the shower and about to get ready for my holiday plans.

"Yeah, right," I tell her, rolling my eyes. Then I sip some of my de-bloating tonic water and wonder if it actually works. Sydney gave it to me yesterday. The both of us have agreed to fast for three days; that way, whatever calories we have on Thanksgiving will balance it out. And then tomorrow morning, I'm going on a ten-mile hike with my bodyguard, since no one else wants to do it with me.

"I'm sorry, I'm sorry," Bee cries. "You have no idea how much homework I have to do like, all the time."

"Boo!" I joke. I've never been into school. I got decent grades when I was a teenager, but I knew the second I graduated, I never wanted to take another test ever again. Thank God, I turned out to be pretty.

Bee and I talk for a few more minutes, then I hang up and make myself look perfect. I'm having Thanksgiving with Shawn and Eliza's family tonight. They were kind enough to invite me when they found out I wasn't going to be going home. If I didn't have their place to hang at so often, I might actually feel lonely enough to go back home for a change. I'm lucky to have them.

Lonnie walks me out of the apartment building and to my car in the parking garage. No one seems to have really figured out where I live yet, so I thankfully don't have to endure the paparazzi and tons of fans eager to spot me.

"You sure you don't want me to drive you?" Lonnie asks, looking concerned. He's my other bodyguard. He and Bryan had to play Rock Paper Scissors over who got to have the holiday off today. I feel bad, but I keep thinking the one day I tell both of them that I'm fine and don't need them is going to be the day I get kidnapped and murdered.

"I'll be fine knowing you're behind me, hot stuff," I tell him with a grin. Lonnie is insanely attractive. I feel like he could be on his way to his big break soon because this guy *needs* to be on TV.

"Alright, then. I'll see you at Shawn and Eliza's." He opens the car door of my lavender-colored Porsche for me, and I get inside. "Don't get lost," he adds as a joke.

I stick my tongue out at him as he closes the door and walks over to the SUV that I have him drive. He knows how bad I am at listening to my map. For some reason, I always think I know a quicker way to get places. I always end up being wrong and frustrated.

I'm not sure what I was expecting when I get to Shawn and Eliza's. I park my car in their circular driveway and get helped out by one of their assistants. I thought there'd be more cars here. More signs of people.

But when I walk inside and head into where I hear the two of them talking to each other in the dining area in front of a massive ceiling-mounted fireplace, I find that no one else is here but them and their workers.

Eliza stands from the table when she sees me. "You look gorgeous!" she tells me.

I am wearing one of her designs because I like when I see her blush. She walks over and gives me a hug. When I wrap my arms around her, I smell something florally and familiar.

"Mm." I breathe in. We pull apart and beam at each other. "You're wearing the perfume I got you!" I cry.

"And you're wearing probably my favorite design of the season," she says back, taking me in and making my stomach dip as her eyes scan my body.

"This is one of yours, Liza?" Shawn asks, standing himself up slowly from his chair to get a look at my outfit. I step around Eliza and pout at Shawn, unable to help it.

"Yes, it is, but don't get up for me, Shawnie." I approach him and wrap my arms around him to give him a hug, and kiss him on the cheek. "It smells amazing in here."

"We didn't cook any of it," Shawn grumbles, sitting back down and taking a sip of some dark-colored liquid in his glass that I'm not sure he should be having.

"But thank you," Eliza finishes for him, retaking her seat as well. Shawn is at the head of the eighteen-person table. Eliza is next to him, so I sit across from her on the other side.

"Belford," Eliza calls to somewhere, then shortly, a man appears. Eliza looks at me. "What would you like to drink?"

"Champagne, please," I reply instinctively. I always go for champagne. It's light.

Shawn grumbles again. "It's Thanksgiving, damn it. Have some eggnog or a chai martini or something for Christ's sake."

I blush. "Well, okay then, chai martini it is!"

The man named Belford nods his head and heads to the bar. In this house, the bar is its own room.

I look around at everything. It's decorated—tastefully—for fall. Jazz music is playing. The fire is going. The way the end of the table is set up looks like something that should be in a holiday magazine. The dishes look expensive. Hell, *everything* looks expensive.

"Do you not normally have a twelve-course meal on Thanksgiving?" Eliza asks, sipping her red wine.

I shake my head. "We set everything up buffet style at my parents' house. Then we eat on TV trays in the living room with football on."

They chuckle. "We used to be like that, too," Shawn explains as my drink comes, and the first course is served. I don't know what I'm looking at on my plate, exactly, but it smells heavenly. "It's funny how quickly things can change."

I'm a nosy person, and I feel comfortable asking the two of them things they might not want to tell me the answer to. So, I ask, "So, uh… is no one else coming?"

Eliza looks at Shawn to answer, and Shawn looks at me like I've just asked something idiotic. "What do you mean?"

"What do you mean, *what do I mean*?" I ask back. "Where's your family? Aren't they coming?" I know Eliza doesn't have any kids of her own, but she's been the stepmom to Shawn's daughter and son for many years.

Shawn stabs his food with his fork and shovels it slowly into his mouth with slightly uncomfortable-looking hands. Now he's too busy to answer me.

Eliza sighs. "Be careful," she snaps at Shawn. She's always worried about him choking since ALS has made swallowing and chewing a difficult task for him. Then she looks back at me. "I told him to invite his kids, but he wanted to have a *quiet* holiday this year."

"That's kind of sad," I can't help but say. "I'm not even your family. You wanted me here instead of them?"

"Not that we don't love you," Eliza tells me, making my heart flutter, "but I said the same thing. He doesn't want to talk to them."

"And I don't want to talk *about* them, either," Shawn says after he finishes his bite.

Eliza gives me a look like she'll explain everything to me later when Shawn isn't around. Butterflies move around in my stomach as I look forward to the opportunity of being alone with her again.

27

DAMASCUS

One year ago…

I excitedly drive up to the fancy, all-white, colonial, gated house in my piece of garbage pick-up truck and send a quick text. I can barely see in through the windows of the home, but the sight makes me want to vomit. Everyone is dressed so *overly* fancy. I can practically *hear* the classical music playing by the four-string quartet in the corner as caterers in black and white outfits walk around and serve fancy hors d'oeuvres and champagne flutes.

It takes only a couple of minutes before I see the front door open and close, Jennifer sneaking out of her house. Then I watch as she runs across the never-ending, perfectly groomed front lawn until she finally reaches the gate and crawls underneath it.

"What do you have there?" I ask her with a grin through my open window as she stands herself up.

She waves a bottle of expensive-looking champagne in front of me. "I snagged it!" she says with a devilish eye wiggle. Then she kisses me through my window and runs to the other side to get in beside me.

"You look cute," I tell her. I want to say she's *stunning* and *incredible*, but I hate everything about how fancy her family made her get just so they could gather with a bunch of people, stuff their faces full of food, and remind themselves about how they stole everything from the Native Americans. It's disgusting and inhumane.

"I sense sarcasm," she tells me as she buckles herself in, shuts the door, and I peel off, hoping to kick up as much dirt as possible in front of their precious iron fence.

"I'm just glad I got you out of there," I say to her with a smirk. I had stayed away from Jennifer as long as I could after I found out whose daughter she was. She just made it too damn impossible. Especially after she told me that she was against everything her father stood for, and that she wanted to help me sabotage his campaign. How was I going to say no to her then? She was basically everything I had ever wanted in a girlfriend.

It's just a shame that her dad ended up winning the election anyway.

"Me, too," Jennifer says dramatically, working to get the cage off of the champagne bottle, her tongue out in concentration.

I chuckle.

"What?" she asks me.

"Nothing." I try and focus on the road and not on her.

"No, what?" she asks again. "Why are you laughing at me?"

"Just that thing you do with your tongue when you're trying really hard. It's cute."

She pouts, and when she resumes trying to open the champagne bottle, I can tell she's concentrating on *not* letting her tongue slip out.

I find somewhere dark and quiet with a clear view of the stars and park the truck.

"What are we doing here?" she asks me, the champagne popping as she finally gets the cork out.

"Come on." I hope out of the truck, and she does the same.

"We're literally in the middle of nowhere. Are you going to murder me or something?"

My sarcasm is thick. "Ha-ha." I walk to the bed of the truck and open the tailgate. Then I turn to Jennifer and reach my hand out. She's staring at the bed of the truck in awe. "You did this… for me?"

I smile sheepishly. "Well… yeah. Of course, I did."

She has to know how crazy about her I am. I know she's crazy about me, too.

The back of my truck is full of blankets, pillows, and battery-operated string lights. I have a bag of Chinese takeout and a cooler full of sodas and bottled water, too. I figured the two of us could cuddle under some blankets, look for shooting stars, and start a new Thanksgiving tradition of our own.

Which is exactly what we end up doing.

28

KENNETH

I don't really know what the point was of me flying back to LA for Thanksgiving. I don't have anyone here to spend the holiday with. No one to cook me a delicious meal and give me leftovers to last me for a week, so I don't have to cook or order takeout for every damn meal.

Luckily for me, though, at least I *do* have someone here whose life is the same exact way. One of my good buddies has no one to spend the holiday with either, unless he feels like flying back home to Virginia, so he's hanging out with me instead.

We're inside some swanky bar called MOST. According to my buddy, it's pretty popular with some well-known female celebrities, and he has his hopes up to get laid tonight.

Currently, the only thing I have my hopes up for is getting drunk, running into my boss, and him telling me I should just stay here and go back to working on more interesting and compelling stories like I've been dreaming of doing ever since I stepped foot in Quincy. I am supposed to be here in LA. Not there. There's a reason I left it in the first place.

"I don't know, man," my buddy says to me, the both of us clinking our glasses of tequila together and drinking the shots. I wince. He doesn't. "There's just something about her. I can't give up that easily."

He's hung up on some chick that he's desperate to be with. She doesn't want him back, but he seems pretty determined to change her mind somehow.

"Do you not see how many other women are here right now?" I try asking him, my voice slurring a little as I point around to the full bar. "You know, most of them have daddy issues since they aren't at home enjoying their Thanksgiving with their family. Come on."

He motions to the bartender that we want another round, even though I really don't. Especially tequila.

What, are we *trying* to kill ourselves or something? I'm not twenty-one anymore.

"I thought I wanted to come here and snag myself

one," my friend says to me. "But the drunker I get, the more I just want to call her, ya know?"

For some reason, my thoughts fly to Selena. I wonder how she is celebrating her Thanksgiving. I really hope she's not home alone with Derek, him opting for a quiet evening in, so no one can hear him mentally and physically abusing her.

"What do you think of Derek Heed?" I ask, completely changing the subject.

My friend makes a disgusted face. "Derek Heed? Do I look like a guy who gives a shit about some college football player?"

"You give enough of a shit to know who he is."

He rolls his eyes. "Because he's trending on Twitter!"

I nod. That damn Twitter. Us Weekly just came out with an entire spread on him. I've been dodging my boss' angry emails. I don't know how to explain to him that it's been a little difficult for me to land any interviews with Derek after our first one went so... swimmingly.

"Well, I don't like him," I say.

"Who cares?"

My buddy apparently has forgotten about why I live in Quincy temporarily, and who I am there trying to get a juicy story on. He only wants to talk about himself.

"Seriously, though," he says, picking up our next round of shots. I do the same. We clink and toss them back. Still, he doesn't wince. "She wouldn't still be texting me and asking to hang out if she didn't feel something, right?"

I want to slap some sense into him. "Forget about her."

"You're no help!"

29

DAMASCUS

Six months ago…

Jennifer and I meet at her coffee shop when she gets off work like we always do. I'm in my truck waiting for her to hop in so we can drive around, make out, and cause mayhem. We've been together for a little over a year now, and it's been the best year of my entire life. No one understands me like Jennifer. Being with her is like being home. She's family. She's my only family. She's all that I have.

When she walks out the back door of the shop, she isn't holding two to-go coffee drinks in her hands like she usually is. Her face is clouded over, too, as she approaches me, and she won't meet my eyes.

"Hey, beautiful," I say to her, trying to sound extra cheery because I can tell that she isn't.

"Dam," she sighs, "can you get out of the truck? We need to talk."

My stomach lurches. Hard. "Why? Is everything okay?" I don't understand what could have happened. Just last night, we were talking on the phone, joking around with each other about the kind of house we want when we are finally able to buy a home together. With her daddy's money, I told her we need to get something fancy.

"Just get out. Please?"

I sigh, turn the truck off, and step out of the vehicle. "Jennifer."

She still won't look at me. I take her chin with my hand, and when I force her to meet my gaze, I nearly jump away from her. Never in our entire relationship have I seen such a cold, vacant expression on her face. It chills me to my core.

She moves her jaw away from my hand. "We need to break up."

Stones drop into my stomach and send it plummeting to my feet. "What the fuck?!"

She crosses her arms and looks deeply into my eyes. She still has the same dead expression, like she could care less about what the words she is saying mean. "I was only with you to get back at my dad."

I feel myself stuttering. My heart is pounding in my ears. "Are you serious?"

"How could you not figure that out? You're everything my dad hates. I wanted to piss him off. You made it easy."

"What are you saying?"

"Are you dumb or something? I don't actually love you. I don't want to be with you. None of this was real."

Blackness starts creeping into the edges of my vision. I'm literally about to pass out right now. "Jennifer. C-come on. Why are you doing this?"

She rolls her eyes. "I just told you! So, go away now, okay? And stop coming back here. I want nothing to do with you."

"I don't fucking believe you!" I shout, tears in my eyes. It kills me that there aren't any in hers, too.

"I don't care!" she shouts back. "I'm with someone else! Someone I actually want to be with!"

I shove her. Not hard, but I just want her out of my face. She stumbles back a little as I turn and jump back inside of my truck and peel out of there as fast as the hunk of metal will allow me.

Her words won't stop replaying in my head. I can't stop seeing the look on her face.

None of it was real.

She's with someone else.

My entire world. Gone in a second.

What the *fuck* am I supposed to do now?

30

DAMASCUS

I want to continue the tradition I started with Jennifer, but I can't risk it making me sad and sending me spiraling again. It's just a shame that what I thought was going to become a tradition of ours only lasted *one* year, because Chinese takeout on the bed of my truck sounds really fucking delicious right now.

I walk around the waterfront of Quincy aimlessly, feeling a familiar urge gnawing inside of me. I hate this stupid holiday. I hate looking in through the windows of families and seeing them celebrating the horrible thing we did to the Native Americans who lived here first. I want to do something… rebellious.

But then I think of Blair. I know she wouldn't appreciate it. I've already mentioned to her about a couple of bad-boy things I've done in the past—she wasn't a fan.

Not that I am letting Blair take control of my decisions now or anything like that. We're not even *like* that; I barely know her. We've hung out a few times, sure. *And* she's incredibly gorgeous, and I can't stop thinking about her, *yes*. But… I don't know. She's just so… different. So *good*. I don't know what the hell she is doing talking to me.

I open the gate that leads to the docks where a bunch of families store their boats. No one seems to be around, and I'm grateful for it. I hop from boat to boat to try and see what personal items of theirs I can take and toss into the ocean. I don't consider it stealing; I just consider it payback for everyone eating their Thanksgiving dinners.

I find a few Bluetooth speakers. Some family photos. Four tablets. Someone's day planner. A really nice set of grilling utensils. The keys to what looks like someone's jet ski. Boat after boat, it seems like I find at least one item I can toss into the water. It makes me feel good. It makes me feel like I am playing my part in trying to right the world.

If only I could find a bigger way to do it.

In one of the boats, I find a kayak attached to it, the paddle inside like it's just waiting for me to take it out, so I do.

When I get far enough, I lean back against my seat and pull out my phone to shoot Blair a text.

Me: *Enjoying your Thanksgiving?*

Blair: *Hardly. What are you up to?*

Me: *Same thing as everyone, I guess. Eating an insane amount of turkey with my family.*

Blair: *Sara told me you boycott Thanksgiving…*

Damn. How much more is Sara going to tell her?

Me: *So, you were asking her about me, huh?*

Blair: *Shut up.*

I laugh and look up at the stars. When I realize I don't have any alcohol on me, I'm actually even happier. I don't remember the last time I terrorized these empty streets without a bottle of something-or-other in my hand. Can it really be because of this Blair chick?

I guess I'm taking too long to say something back to her text because a few minutes later, my phone buzzes on my chest again.

Blair: *When are we hanging out?*

Me: *Now would be pretty cool.*

My stomach dips when it takes her longer than I expected to reply. I stare hard at my phone screen in my hand, hoping I didn't come off too strong. I don't want her to think I'm clingy.

Blair: *I wish. My parents are super strict on family time.*

But I'm satisfied enough. At least she admitted she wants to.

I continue to look up at the stars, unable to help the thoughts now flowing through me. I don't know what it is. But something about Blair makes me feel like she might become a huge part of my life.

31

BRENNAN

"I feel like we haven't done this in forever," I say to Derek.

We're at Henderson's, getting drunk together, just the two of us. He has the entire weekend off for Thanksgiving, and luckily for me, Selena wanted to go spend some time with her girlfriends or something tonight, and Derek wanted to get drunk with his little brother, I guess.

"I know, we really should hang more often," Derek

says to me. He's not nearly as drunk as I am yet, but we've had about the same amount of alcohol to drink.

"I mean, you live so close to us, and I never see you!" I complain, sounding like Mom.

"You sound like Mom," Derek says, hearing it, too. We both laugh. "When are you going to get a place of your own, anyway?"

I shrug. I'm not really in any hurry to leave Mom and Dad's, as annoying as it can get to be there sometimes. I keep myself busy enough with my sports shop and my bars and my buddies. I'm not even home much, and it's saving me a fortune on rent.

I was able to get out of the lease I had with Brielle, and she told me her parents are going to help her pay for the other half of her rent until the lease ends, and she moves somewhere else—probably Travis' house.

Derek nudges my forearm with his. "Let's go play some golf." He's not referring to actual golf; there's an arcade game in the corner of the bar where you use this rolling ball to shoot golf balls as far as you can. Not much skill is required, so it makes it the perfect drinking game.

We head over to it, and Derek goes first.

"You have to get out of there eventually," Derek continues our conversation from up at the bar. "You're like, what, twenty-five now?"

"Twenty-six."

"Dude. You're not even thirty, and you *own* a company. That's insane!" Derek takes a large gulp of his IPA. His favorite beer, same as me. "You should be buying *my* drinks."

"Like you're not making money off of your social media and OnlyFans," I joke. The only reason that I own my own company is because I got the job at Go Play as a high schooler, and the owner at the time, Allen Mason, had three daughters and no son or nephew to hand it off to when he retired.

Brennan punches my bicep after rolling the ball on the machine as hard as he can. The golf ball flies far and lands nearly right next to the hole.

Go figure.

I step up to go next, but I take my time choosing my character's outfit, shoes, and club. I know it drives Derek nuts.

"I don't have an OnlyFans," he tells me.

I laugh and sip my drink. "That's not what your old girlfriend told me."

"Which one?" Derek sounds defensive.

"Dude. I'm joking."

"Selena would kill me if I had one of those," he goes on. Then he angrily throws in, "Dude, hurry up already!" because I still haven't rolled the ball to hit my golf ball. I already know it's not going to go nearly as far as his did. Derek is basically better than me at everything we do.

"How are you two doing, by the way?" I ask him about his wife, hoping that he'll tell me she's evil, and he hates her, and he's hoping to get a divorce soon. Now that I am finally single again, I want him to be single with me. We could have so much fun hitting up downtown Quincy on the weekends and meeting up with all kinds of college chicks.

At least for a little while until it gets boring, and I find myself missing being in a relationship again—although I don't know how the fuck I am ever going to find someone else to be with in this small town.

I finally take my turn, and the ball surprisingly gets a lot closer to the hole than I thought it would, but it's still not as good as Derek's shot.

Derek snickers and shoves me out of the way, clearly eager for it to be his turn again. "Things are great, man."

My heart sinks. "That's good," I lie.

"Yeah. I love her, ya know? Marrying her is the best decision I ever made. I mean, I know all these other chicks want me now and whatnot." He takes his shot and moves over for me to go. "Like, Brennan—even *famous* girls want me. It's insane, seriously. I bet I could introduce you to some. Give them your Instagram."

"No, thanks," I say. Famous women sound a little too high maintenance for me.

"Suit yourself."

"So, you're still happy with her? Even with all the other temptations?" I can't help but wonder if he ever cheats on Selena. I guess after being cheated on myself recently, it's something I ponder often. Does everyone cheat on their significant other? Is every single relationship in the entire world doomed?

Derek looks at me like I'm being a jackass. "Yeah, dude. I'd never jeopardize our marriage."

I finish my drink as Derek gets his ball into the hole and wins the round.

"I'm going to get us more," I tell him, turning and walking back over to Jane behind the bar. It's nice hanging with Derek like this, and I don't even know why I feel like I'm in such a crappy mood all of a sudden. It's like I'm annoyed that his life is so much more perfect than mine. I should be happy for him, not hoping that his life will fall apart with mine.

Maybe I'll feel better if I can just win *one* round of golf.

32

KENNETH

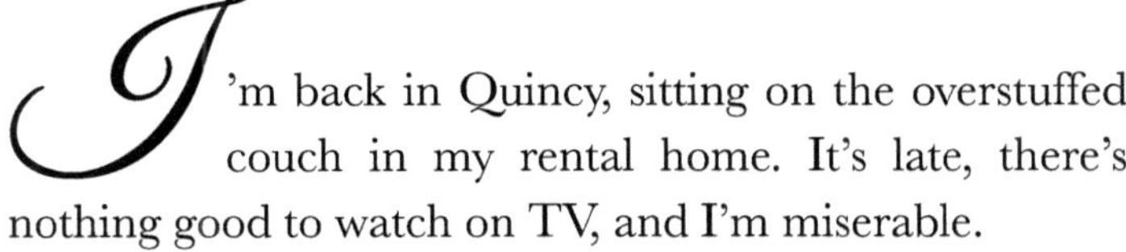

I'm back in Quincy, sitting on the overstuffed couch in my rental home. It's late, there's nothing good to watch on TV, and I'm miserable.

A knock makes me jump in my seat, the glass of milk in my hand spilling out the top of it and getting all over my hand, arm, and dripping onto the sofa.

Who could that be?

I get up and walk toward the door, checking the time on my watch as I go—it's after midnight.

I look through the peephole, expecting to find some annoying kids playing a prank on me, or to find no one because the prank they're playing is Ding Dong Ditch—it's happened before.

What I'm not expecting is to see the person who actually *is* standing outside on my front porch right now.

I unlock and open the door.

"Selena?"

She is turned around, her back to me like she is looking to make sure no one had followed her here. When she turns back around to face me, I see the black eye, and I see that she's crying.

"You were right," she says simply, letting her hands drop by her sides.

"Oh… crap, what happened?"

She sniffs. "Do you think I can maybe come in?"

I step aside quickly. Of course, I want her in my crappy house and not out where Derek might be able to see that she came here. I close the door and lock it again when she's safely inside.

"Thanks," she replies, sniffing again and slowly turning herself around to check out my place. "I'm sorry to come here like this. I know it was stupid of me, and I know you probably hate me."

I shake my head at her. "Let me get you some ice." I walk three steps to my freezer and pull out the ice tray. When I smack it against the counter to loosen up the pieces, Selena flinches.

"Are you okay?" I ask her. "Do you want me to call the police?" I can't believe Derek Heed punched her. He actually punched her! She has the marks to prove it, too.

"No!" she snaps, looking horrified. "You can't, Kenneth. Please."

I drop some pieces of ice into a zipped plastic bag and hand it to her. "Why? Hold that against your eye and sit down. But not on the couch. You scared the shit out of me, and I spilled my drink."

"Is that… milk?" she asks, seeing my glass on the end table as she holds the ice to her eye and sits on the chair at my small dining table.

"What?" I ask defensively. "What's wrong with milk?"

To my amazement, she giggles. Derek Heed just punched her in the face, and now she's in my rental giggling with a black eye.

"Um, I didn't know grown men still drink it," she explains. But how *could* she know? She's only ever been with *Derek* since she became an adult.

"Oh, Derek might not, but the rest of us definitely do," I joke, picking up my glass and taking a huge gulp out of it. When I pull it away from my lips, I hope I have a large milk mustache because I think it might help get her to stop crying.

She giggles quietly and shakes her head as she watches me. I wipe the 'stache, put the cup in the sink, and wet a cloth with warm water and dish soap to go clean the mess.

"Cute house," she says to me with another pitiful sniff.

"Selena, why don't you want me to call the cops? That jackass needs to pay for what he did to you."

"It's so complicated, Kenneth. You have no idea."

"You need to take a photo of it, at least. Right now, while it's fresh. And you need to document the time and place it happened, and everything you two said to each other. Don't leave out any detail. Not even your clothes."

Selena is wearing her pajamas. She clearly had to run out of her house quickly, so afraid that Derek was going to do something else that she couldn't even bring herself to chance taking the time to pack a bag. It makes me sick to my stomach.

"What are you, a cop or something?" she asks me.

"I'm a journalist," I remind her, scrubbing and dabbing my couch. "One who is here looking for a story on Derek Heed, too."

"It can't be about this," she snaps.

I internally groan. She *would* ask me not to expose him. I don't get her.

I have to ask. "So, then why are you here?"

She sighs heavily and gets back to her feet. I think her tears have finally subsided. She pulls the ice away from her eye. I take my phone out, turn the camera on, and step toward her.

"Let me?" I ask.

She sticks her bad side out a little so I can get a clear picture, then she explains herself. "I don't know anyone else in this town except for the guys on the team. I met Derek in college. My family lives super far away."

I hand her my phone—it has a composed text message open with the picture on it, the phone number space blank so that she can type in her number and send it to herself. She does so without asking questions.

"Do you not have any friends here?" I ask. "Anyone you can trust?"

"No," she admits. "Derek literally doesn't let me have friends. He doesn't let me do anything ever. He's a terrible human being. The main reason I came to you is because I know you agree with me. Derek's own family wouldn't even listen to me if I were to try and explain this to them."

I race over to my notebook and jot down, *Derek's family*. I need to talk to them.

"That's horrible," I say, closing the notebook and putting the pen down. "Put the ice back on your eye."

She does as she's told and hands me my phone back. It vaguely hits me that I now have her cell number.

"Yeah. It is."

I run a hand through my hair and try to think of what I can do for her. I don't exactly have the extra money to buy her a hotel room somewhere, and even if I did, I wouldn't feel comfortable not knowing if she was safe there or not.

"Okay, so how about I don't ask you any other questions, and we don't talk about it anymore for the rest of the night?" I decide. "Just crash here, and we will figure things out tomorrow. Does that sound good?"

She looks uncertain.

"I even have an extra toothbrush," I try. "I forgot to pack one, and when I went to the store, they only had a two-pack."

She gives me the tiniest hint of a smile.

Good, we're getting somewhere.

33

GISELLE

I am here at Eliza's office again because she requested my assistance. Steve is here, too—Eliza wants him to take some preliminary shots of me in the designs she's been working on. I've basically been her personal mannequin for her entire process, so it was only fitting that I be in these photos so Eliza can flip through them easily on her own time and decide on which ones she wants to move forward with.

It's been a long morning so far, and it's surely going

to turn into a long afternoon, too. Eliza has come up with fifty-five outfits. She needs to select a final portion of about an *eighth* of that.

"I don't get how she is ever going to choose," Steve jokes to me as he takes my photos against a simple black backdrop in a room at Eliza's office building.

It's a warehouse-like space meant for occasions just like this—like it's one great testing room. Fabric samples lay strewn about. Overflow storage items are in large bins and boxes on tall metal shelving units. Endless racks of clothing are lined up along one of the walls. There's even a plain white runway that goes down the middle of the room.

"What do you mean?" I ask through my poses, switching it up. Eliza wants me in about five poses per outfit. I just keep moving and following Steve's instructions in hopes that they will be to Eliza's liking.

"You've looked amazing in every single thing so far," Steve compliments.

Normally, I would have been flattered and appreciative of his words, but now I just feel uncomfortable. I know that Steve likes me as more than a friend, and I know I still want to keep him as a friend even though I don't feel the same way, and *yes*, I said things didn't have to be all weird between us now, but I don't know… I guess it still *is* weird. It's all his fault! He made it weird. I think I might be mad at him a bit for it.

Eliza enters the room when I am on outfit twenty-two. It's a simple black dress with short sleeves and a slit up the right thigh. I'm a big fan of it, and I've told her so several times.

At the sight of me, Eliza's eyes don't brighten like they normally do. She doesn't even smile. She just walks over in her elegant linen pants and shapely chocolate-colored top, and stands next to Steve to observe me silently with her arms crossed. Now suddenly, I feel uncertain and uncomfortable. I may be at ease around Steve when shooting, but it's because I know he finds me attractive no matter what. I want to impress Eliza, and right now, it doesn't really feel like I am doing that.

Eliza stands there a whole three minutes before I see the faraway look in her eyes. She's not even watching me. I can tell her mind is somewhere else entirely.

"Giselle?" Steve asks me, breaking my thoughts apart and getting me to focus back on him.

"Hm?"

"You're doing that weird thing with your jaw. Relax."

I loosen my jaw and try to get back to focusing on my poses, not on Eliza.

But when Eliza puts a hand over her mouth suddenly and turns around and nearly runs out of the room—her heels echoing loudly on the cement floor and her long, white, and blonde hair flowing freely behind her—I stop posing altogether, and Steve stops taking pictures. We both turn and look after her.

"Is she okay?" Steve asks.

I have never seen her do anything like this.

Unsure if she hates me, the clothes, or is upset about something *else*, I step off of the backdrop and stare at Steve with confused eyes. "I have no idea."

I know he's known her longer than I have, but I still

have a feeling I know her better, and that it should be me who chases after her to see what's going on—even if she's going to fire me or tell me to start from the beginning and change my poses.

"Should we just keep going?" Steve asks, holding his camera up to me.

"Uh, I'll be right back." I leave Steve and walk out the same doors that Eliza had just gone out of. Out in the hall, I see there are three places she could have gone —the woman's room, the stairwell, or the custodial closet. I don't even bother checking the custodial closet because I highly doubt I would find her there. I go to the woman's restroom first, but no one is inside. So, I head to my last option: the stairwell.

I open the heavy metal door and immediately hear the sound of someone sobbing. If it's Eliza crying, that's going to be another thing I have never seen her do. I creep over to the railing on the landing I'm on and peer down. Eliza is only one set of stairs below me, her head in her hands and her shoulders shaking.

"Eliza?"

I take off down the stairs to reach her. At the sound of my voice, she quickly sniffs, wipes her eyes, and stands up straighter. "Oh, I'm sorry, Giselle."

Her bloodshot eyes made my stomach twist. I hate seeing her like this.

I don't know if she wants to be hugged or left alone, so I just stand there and don't do either.

"What happened?" I ask. "If you hate me in this, or hate my poses, or whatever it is, you can tell me. I can take it."

She shakes her head and sniffs again. "It's not any of that. The dress is beautiful. You're… beautiful." She looks me directly in the eyes when she speaks, and it makes my heart catch in my throat. I take her hand.

"Then what is it?"

She sighs heavily. "It's… Oh, it's Shawn. It's the damn ALS. I'm so sorry. I'm usually much stronger about all of this. I don't know what's gotten into me."

I hug her now because the fact that her husband is dying of an unforeseen, incurable disease is something that anyone would want to be hugged over. To my relief, she accepts the comfort graciously and squeezes me back tightly.

"Did something happen?" I ask into her ear, not letting her go.

"It's just progressing quicker than we all had hoped. It's just all so… hard. On the both of us."

We slowly pull our heads away from each other, but she doesn't remove her hands from my waist, and I don't remove mine from around her shoulders.

She continues. "I just feel so…"

I realize that our noses are only centimeters away from touching. I stand there and wait for Eliza to finish her sentence, but instead, her eyes flutter to my lips, then she leans in and kisses me.

34

BRENNAN

It's not my alarm clock that wakes me up this morning. Instead, my eyes snap open at the sound of my mom whining in a high-pitched, loud, shrill tone. It's not a voice of hers I hear often, so I throw my comforter off of me, leave my bedroom, and step out into the hall.

"Who, Richard? Who?!" Mom is saying. I step toward the banister and lean over to hear better. It sounds like she and my father are in the kitchen.

"I don't know, Laur! It's all lies. As long as the people close to him know that, none of it matters," Dad says to her. I have no idea what it is they could possibly be talking about.

"It's not all that matters!" Mom argues with him. "This could ruin him, Rich! He doesn't deserve this! He hasn't done anything wrong!"

Okay, now I have to know what's going on.

I step quickly down the stairs, jumping over the bottom two like I usually do. Mom and Dad stop talking when they hear my footsteps, and when I enter the kitchen, they're both looking at me.

"What's going on?" I ask. "I could hear you yelling from upstairs, Ma."

She shakes her head and puts it in her hands. She and my father are both leaning against the counter at opposite sides of the room. "Have you seen the news? Or social media, or whatever the hell it's been posted on?"

"Whatever the hell *what's* been posted on?" I ask, still barely awake as I scratch the top of my bedhead. "I just woke up."

"I don't even want you to look at it," Mom says. "I don't want to give it any more attention. It doesn't *need* any more attention because... well, it's just not true!" She looks pretty close to tears now.

My heart starts beating faster. "Tell me what's going on."

Dad sighs and sips his coffee. "Someone anonymously posted a rumor about Derek."

"A lie!" Mom corrects.

Dad nods. "Well, yes, sorry. A lie."

"About?"

"Oh my gosh, what are people going to think? What are they going to say to me?" Mom goes on, talking to herself more than to anyone else.

"It'll be fine, Laurie. Stop worrying so much, okay?" Dad tries.

"No!"

My eyes widen. Mom sounds like a toddler throwing a tantrum. "What's the rumor—sorry!—lie?" I ask, correcting myself when Mom throws me a furious look. I'm terrified to hear what is about to come out of her mouth. I have no idea what to expect.

"Someone said that Derek is an abusive partner. They posted it on social media under an anonymous account. Twitter and Instagram, I think," Dad finally explains.

Instantly, my blood begins to boil.

"And it spread like wildfire overnight," Mom adds. "It's on the news now! Everyone is talking about it! You should've heard Derek on the phone this morning. He's a mess… it's horrible!"

I already have an idea of who could have done this. My mind instantly flies to one person. One whom I dislike. Whom I've always disliked.

"Do you think Selena posted it?" I ask, expecting her to be the type to do such a thing.

But I can't believe she would stoop this low. I can't believe she is even more of a terrible person than I thought her to be. She could ruin Derek's entire future with an accusation like this.

It's messed up, and there's no possible way she's telling the truth. My brother would never. No one in this family would ever.

"Derek doesn't think so. The person who posted about him referred to herself as his ex," Mom says.

I just don't buy it. With this lie being spread out there, I already know this family is about to go through much turmoil. Hard times are ahead. Not just for Derek, but for all of us. I can taste it.

All because of a lie.

Because that's what this is—a lie.

Dad sips his coffee again. "And we all know how many girlfriends he's had. Who knows who posted it…"

"They just want attention," Mom says. "It makes me sick. They could ruin his life with this! Everything he's worked so hard toward!"

I sit down at the counter and motion for Dad to pour me a cup out of the coffee pot he's standing next to. My head hurts from thinking about this so early in the morning.

"Is Derek okay?" I ask.

Dad pours the coffee and slides it across the counter to me. It's scalding hot when it touches my tongue.

"He's worried, which is understandable," Mom tells me. She has a cup of coffee next to her, too, but she isn't touching it. "We're trying to figure out if this person just wants money. Fame? Attention? We want to know how to make this all go away."

"I mean, whoever said it is clearly lying, right?" I want to make sure we're all on the same page about this. It's just not true. It could never be true.

"Scouts won't be looking at him while this is circulating around the media. It would make them look bad," Dad says, ignoring my question.

"This is *not* good," Mom says. "Not good at all."

Who could have done this to Derek if it wasn't his own wife?

"Have you talked to Selena?" I ask them. "What's she doing about all of this? Anything to dispel the lies and say they're not true?"

"Derek was advised to tell Selena not to," Dad says. "Not yet, anyway. They don't want it to look like she was instructed to do so. The quicker she defends him, the higher the risk that it'll look bad, I suppose."

I stretch on my stool, still trying to wake myself up a bit. "Is there anything I can do?" I want to be able to help my brother get out of this mess. He doesn't deserve this. His future could be ruined over this. All of our futures could be.

And I can't help but feel like a complete jerk. I had been so rude to him last weekend, envious that his life was going so well. For some stupid reason, I almost feel like my negative thoughts caused this to happen to him.

"Just give him a call and let him know you're on his side," Dad tells me. "I'm sure he'd appreciate hearing that from you right now."

I nod my head and stand. Of course, I'm on his side. He's my older brother. He's the person I've always admired and looked up to. If he really is an abusive person, wouldn't I have figured that out by now?

I have to get him out of this mess.

164

The End

HALLOWEEN HEARTBREAK

BOOK ONE OF THE MISSED CONNECTIONS TRILOGY

KATHRYN REIGN